ONE PASS AWAY
BOOK ONE

AFTER THE RAIN

MARY J. WILLIAMS

ABOUT THE AUTHOR

Want to know how to motivate yourself to write a book? Have your favorite football team lose the Super Bowl. On the last play. With an interception. The next day I was so depressed I tuned out all media. No TV, no internet, no newspapers — nothing. And I started to write. I'm still writing. As you can see, a little motivation can do wonders. Football is the center of my next series of books. And since I'm writing the ending? No interceptions. Guaranteed. Happy reading everyone.

Mary J. Williams

HOW TO GET IN TOUCH

Please visit me at these sites, sign up for my newsletter, or leave a message.

http://www.maryjwilliams.net/home.html

https://www.facebook.com/pages/Mary-J-Williams/1561851657385417

https://twitter.com/maryjwilliams05

https://www.pinterest.com/maryj0675/

https://www.goodreads.com/author/show/5648619.Mary_J_Williams

MORE BOOKS BY MARY J. WILLIAMS

__Harper Falls Series__
If I Loved You
If Tomorrow Never Comes
If You Only Knew
If I Had You (Christmas in Harper Falls)

__Hollywood Legends__
Dreaming With A Broken Heart

TABLE OF CONTENTS

PROLOGUE

LOGAN. LOGAN. LOGAN.

Logan Price closed his eyes, taking it all in.

"Hear that, kid?" Starting quarterback Gaige Benson slapped him on the back. "Two games under your belt and you're a star. Now let's go out there and add super to the front of it."

The announcer for the team set them in motion down the tunnel with his familiar introduction.

"And now, let's hear it for your division champion *SEATTLE KNIGHTS.*"

The roar of the crowd. There was nothing like it. A packed stadium. Fans chanting his name. Few people would ever experience what it was like to take the field in a professional football game.

Logan Price had been working for his entire life. He could still remember in exact detail the first game he ever saw. Too small to climb onto the stool in his father's bar by himself, his old man had lifted him onto the seat.

Stay and be quiet.

Not an easy order to follow for an active, inquisitive little boy. One look at the game and for once, Logan had no problem following his father's command. The old TV transported him to a foreign world filled with bright lights and shiny helmeted warriors. Logan didn't know what he was watching. He did know he wanted to be one of those men.

A Sunday afternoon in rural Oklahoma. *Lefty's Pub* was filled with after-church drinkers who figured they had done their duty to God and family. The rest of the day was their time. A beer. Or two. Or six.

Cronies who understood a man's need to unwind before the start of another workweek.

And football.

If the Friday night high school game was their true religion, the Sunday afternoon games were a close second. As Oklahoma boys, they hated anything Texas. The men of Denville gathered every week to root for whichever team was playing the Dallas Cowboys.

No matter how the games ended. Whether the crowd was happy or disgruntled. It meant more drinking. Hours later, husbands, boyfriends, and sons would stumble out, pile into beat-up trucks, and weave their way home to frustrated wives, girlfriends, and mothers.

As he grew older, Logan's view changed. He moved from the stool to behind the bar. And he promised himself one thing. He would never become one of those men. He wouldn't spend the week at a job he hated. His home wouldn't be a semi-wide trailer filled with hand-me-down furniture and a wife to whom he couldn't face going home.

His Sundays were going to be spent playing football, not watching it.

"Ready to take down this vaunted Arizona defense?" Gaige yelled at him, butting helmets.

Vaunted. Good word, Logan thought. His QB liked to use what his granny called highfalutin talk. Must have been that Ivy League education. He knew that Gaige Benson didn't grow up with a silver spoon in his mouth. He came from the mean streets of Brooklyn. He had the scars to prove it.

Like Logan, Gaige had vowed to get out of the life into which he was born. In the process, he polished himself up like a new penny. He took advantage of his full-ride scholarship to Yale. He didn't spend all his time on the football field. Fancy vocabulary. Fancy clothes. Fancy women. They were all part of the package Gaige purposefully fashioned for himself.

Seventeen years after clawing his way out of the tenement that he grew up in, very little of that borough-rat remained. Until game time. No one was tougher than Gaige Benson. Three-time league MVP. Considered one of the best ever to play the game. No one stood in his way when he was playing the game. He had the scars to prove it.

"Gather round."

Knights head coach Harry Coleman gathered the team close. He had to yell over the crowd, but he had the voice to do it. Booming was putting it mildly. The first time Logan heard it he stood right beside the man. The ringing in his ears didn't go away for three days.

"Divisional game. If I have to say any more than that, you shouldn't be out here. Go kick some ass."

The defense took the field to start the game. Arizona had a rookie quarterback drafted in the second round from a small college in the Midwest. The only reason he was out there was because the regular starter suffered a concussion in last week's game and the regular backup had food poisoning. Thrown into action at the last minute, Logan swore he could see the guy's hands shaking before he took the first snap. When the ball went sailing between his legs, Logan shook his head.

The moment was too big for some people. For Logan, it wasn't big enough. He aimed for the biggest stage of all. The Super Bowl. It wasn't a matter of *if* he would get there, but when.

"Three and out." Gaige grinned, pulling on his helmet. "Come on, kid. Let's go show them how it's done."

Logan ran onto the field. *Kid.* He shook his head, grinning. From the first day of training camp, Gaige had hung that moniker on him. Ironic since he was almost twenty-five, a good two years older than most of the other rookies. However, he supposed when someone had been in the league as long as Gaige, all the new guys seemed like kids.

"We're starting on the ground," Gaige instructed them in the huddle. "Sweep out left. Basic. Got it?"

Lining up as he had a thousand other times, Logan checked the defense. He knew he was fast. One of the fastest in the game. What set him apart was his anticipation. He had the uncanny ability to read the guy covering him. He knew when to fake left or when to fake right. Stutter step or flat out, in your face, catch me if you can.

His speed got him out of Denville, Oklahoma. His brains and determination got him to the NFL.

The sounds of the game were as familiar to Logan as the back of his own hand. The call from scrimmage. Each quarterback had his own unique cadence. Gaige was a master of mixing his up. Study him all you want. Good luck figuring it out. His teammates knew. A signal just before they broke the huddle.

Pay attention, you were golden. Slack off even once? Gaige could ream a guy out with the best of them. And he had no problem doing it in the middle of the game.

An entire YouTube channel had been devoted to Gaige and his

rants. They were as legendary as the man himself. With a ball in his hand, he was cool as ice. The rest of the time, watch out.

No one would ever accuse Logan of lacking focus. Today was no exception. They were driving down the field. First and ten from the Arizona twenty-yard line. He already had three carries of thirty-five yards. It was going to be a good day.

"Ready to take it in?" Gaige asked.

"Always."

"Then show them what you've got."

A quick snap later, Gaige handed the ball to Logan. The offensive line created a seam. Not a big one. Just big enough. Using the push of his powerful legs, Logan surged through. One more step. They wouldn't catch him. No one could.

Like everything connected with the game, Logan heard the snap of the bone with total clarity. The agony that surged through his body was so intense he almost passed out. In the next few minutes, he was going to wish he had.

"Get back." Logan heard Gaige through the haze of pain. "Goddamn it. Move the hell off."

The three-hundred-and-fifty-pound linebacker didn't get off by standing. He rolled. Crushing Logan's broken leg as he went. He would never know if the move had been deliberate. Now, it was the last thing on his mind. He only cared about two things. How bad was the injury and when would he be able to play again.

"Hold on, kid." Gaige took his hand. "They're bringing the stretcher."

The team doctor checked his eyes. Logan knew he was asked some questions. What they were and how he answered, he would never remember. By the time they carted him off the field, Logan knew the break was bad.

"Gaige." Logan reached for him.

"I'm here, kid."

"Is it over?"

"The game?" Gaige walked with him, his head bent toward Logan. "No. But I promise we're going to win the bastard."

They loaded him onto the open cart. They had him secured and the vehicle rolled away before Logan had his answer. He wasn't wondering about the game. It was his career.

To no one in particular, he whispered the question again.

"Is it over?"

CHAPTER ONE

L OGAN SAT UP in bed, his body covered with a fine coating of sweat.

He glanced at the clock. Three in the fucking morning. On the one night he managed to get to bed at a reasonable hour, he was plagued by the nightmare that had haunted his dreams for the past two years.

Running his hand through his long, damp hair, Logan fell back onto the mattress. His sheets were as wet as he was. With a grimace, he rolled onto the floor. Flexing his stiff knee, he stripped the bed, tossing everything onto a pile of dirty clothes he planned on taking to the laundromat on his day off.

There was an alternative. He could always take Linda Sue Hemmings up on her offer. She would do his laundry anytime. Payment. On-call stud service whenever her husband Darryl was out of town on business. As much as Logan hated folding socks, he decided the price was too high. He had lost a lot in the last few years. He still held onto his dignity. Just barely.

Still groggy, Logan shuffled to the bathroom. Flipping on the light, he grimaced at what the mirror reflected.

Too many late nights followed by not enough sleep. As patterns went, it wasn't a healthy one. Perpetually bloodshot eyes. Dark circles on his dark circles. He needed a haircut. Logan ran his hand over his face. Even more, he needed a shave.

He had to hand it to himself. When he let himself go, he went all the way. All he had to do was stop showering. If he wasn't worried about driving the customers away with his smell, he might have considered it.

The old plumbing rattled with protest when he turned on the faucet. It wasn't a bad place. There were worse. Logan splashed some cold water on his face. He didn't bother with a towel. It would dry soon enough on its own.

He had two choices.

Toss and turn for a couple of hours on the unmade bed – he really needed to get more than one set of sheets.

Or lose himself with an old friend.

Sleep wasn't coming which made the choice an easy one.

Logan pulled on a pair of old shorts, a faded t-shirt and sweatshirt that was too ratty to be called anything as fashionable as a hoodie. After lacing up his sneakers, he hit the road. When he was a kid, he ran for the fun of it. In high school and college, it strengthened his legs and improved his stamina. Now, the only thing it accomplished was getting him a reputation as that half-crazy Price boy. Running the deserted streets at all hours? Maybe his head had been permanently injured along with his leg.

Logan jogged past *Lefty's Pub*. The place where he spent most evenings tending bar. The day he left for college he swore to anyone who would listen that he had served his last beer. Eight years later, here he was, washing glasses and putting up with not so subtle jabs about how the mighty had fallen.

Coming back to Denville was more of an adjustment than Logan anticipated. He expected the cracks about his failed NFL career. Any kind of success tended to breed a certain amount of jealousy and resentment. There were those who reveled in his injury.

Logan Price always thought too much of himself. Denville wasn't good enough for the high school's star running back. He forgot all about us when he made it big.

The sound of his feet pounding on the unpaved side street couldn't keep the usual thoughts from creeping back. Some of what those people said was true. He had been full of himself. At seventeen, one wasn't written up in national magazines without it going to his head.

Logan never tried to hide his plans. A full-ride scholarship to the college of his choice. Then the pros. MVP awards. Super Bowl rings. The cocky attitude of a teenager wasn't any easier to take than if he had been an adult. Most of Denville embraced their golden boy.

Then there were the ones who didn't. The ones who occupied the same table at *Lefty's Pub* every Saturday night and Sunday afternoon. Led by Rafer Macafee, their sole purpose was to drink as much cheap beer as possible. The bonus was goading Logan.

Rafer hated Logan from way back. Before they played on the same high school team. Why, Logan couldn't really say. One of those cases of instant dislike – on both sides. They had been rivals. Basketball, baseball, football. The seasons and the sports changed. The antagonism never did.

Early on, he and Rafer were equal in ability. Each had his strength. Logan's outside shot was a killer. Inside the paint, Rafer couldn't miss. Rafer had the better fastball, but Logan hit more home runs. On the gridiron, Rafer knocked down the opposition with brutal glee. Logan used his speed to win games.

The separation started sophomore year. Something happened to their growing bodies. Logan shot up while Rafer sagged out. Along with his new height, Logan added muscle. Using the money he made doing odd jobs around town, he drove his father's truck fifty miles each way, three days a week, to the nearest gym. If he wanted to be taken seriously by recruiters, weight training was essential. Fast was great. Fast and strong was better.

Rafer, on the other hand, had no ambition. He used his growing size to push around smaller bodies on and off the field. After high school, he planned on marrying Janna Lindstrom, working in his family's seed and feed, and being a bully. Why change what worked for you?

Turned out, Rafer's lack of big plans didn't stop him from harboring resentment over Logan's. Rafer was always the first to point out how much the odds were against a nothing running back from a backwater town. Who the hell was going to notice Logan's gaudy stats? When the national press started to do just that, Rafer's hate and resentment grew.

Logan was too caught up in his own world to worry about Rafer Macafee. Everything was going as planned. In a year, he would graduate. Logan Price planned to celebrate his nineteenth birthday as a member of the Alabama Crimson Tide. He didn't doubt for a moment his dream school would come calling. And they did.

Logan was on his way. Then the unthinkable happened. His father had a heart attack. For years, it had been just the two of them. His mother died when Logan was three. No brothers or sisters. Not aunts or uncles. Jonas Price did what had to be done. He brought his son up with a firm hand and a loving heart. A heart that turned out to need a triple bypass.

There was no way he could leave his father. Someone had to take care of him and the bar. There was no one else. Logan's dreams would have to wait. He gave up his scholarship and stayed in Denville.

Friends were sympathetic. Rafer Macafee rubbed it in Logan's face every chance he got.

Eighteen and already washed up.

Logan didn't respond. This time, he kept his plans to himself. He didn't consider it the end, only a slight detour.

The first thing Logan did was volunteer to be an assistant coach for the high school team. Money was always tight in Denville, so they jumped at the chance. Free and a local legend? They would be crazy to turn that down.

Logan saw it as his chance to stay connected to the game. He worked out hard with the team, staying in shape. Not that it was all about him. He didn't slack in his duties. Most of the players knew him. He was only a season removed from taking them to the state championship. The connection was already there.

For the next year, Logan worked his ass off to keep *Lefty's Pub* running and his dreams on track. All the hard work paid off when his father returned, the doctors giving him a clean bill of health.

The scholarship to Alabama was a thing of the past – the school had moved on to the next big high school sensation. Undeterred, Logan tried out for every college that would agree to see him. In the end, he received three offers. Logan chose Ohio State. If a big national powerhouse like the Buckeyes wanted to take a chance on a man who would turn twenty during the season, Logan planned to take advantage of the opportunity.

The team redshirted him that first season. The head coach saw his potential and decided a year of seasoning would be best for all involved. Logan didn't argue. He considered whatever he received to be gravy. He would work his ass off for the man who believed enough to give him his second chance.

Five years later, Logan went as the first pick in the second round of the NFL draft to the Seattle Knights. A tidy if not spectacular signing bonus that he promptly used to pay off his father's old medical bills and the mortgage on his childhood home. What was left he directly gave to his father. A small thank you for all his support and encouragement.

The injury in his third game as a pro halted his vision of a future filled with wealth and fame in its tracks. Logan Price wasn't a has-been.

He qualified as a lowly never was. No one shelled out money for endorsement deals to bartenders in Denville, Oklahoma.

What little money he had made was gone. He lived over a garage with old plumbing and insulation that barely kept out the mid-December wind.

Listening to the taunts from a bunch of drunks was the least of his problems.

Not that it didn't burn at first. His retirement had been recent enough that the words cut into his pride and ego. Now, over a year later, Logan no longer paid attention to Rafer and his cronies.

Was it a sign his skin had thickened? Or that he was sinking further into his *I no longer give a crap about anything* existence? At four in the morning, Logan couldn't have cared less.

Someday he would find the balance between what might have been and the here and now. Knowing that day would come scared the shit out of him. Giving up had never been in his DNA, but it was creeping in – inch by depressing inch.

When he felt his body reaching the end of its endurance, instead of heading home, Logan turned into the parking lot at *Lefty's Pub*. There were always things to do. Floors to mop. Liquor to inventory. That top shelf of glasses hadn't been taken down for a good cleaning in a while. Busy work.

Logan fished out the keys from his pocket, letting himself into the darkened bar. Pitch black except for one beer sign from an old brand that wasn't made anymore. His father never turned that one off.

An old warhorse, Jonas Price called it. Just like him. On the day he took his last breath, the sign would come down. A little morbid? Maybe. Logan planned to do his damnedest to make sure they both kept shining for a long, long time.

Logan flipped on the light over the bar. Checking the bottles, the decision was made for him. Time to restock. With the smell of stale beer filling his nose, he unlocked the door to the basement where the extra stock was stored.

Logan sighed. A few more hours until dawn. And then…? Another day like all the rest. One foot in front of the other.

"WHAT DO YOU think?"

"Besides questioning why we're sitting in a freezing car, in Nowhere, Oklahoma, watching a man jog through town?"

"Ya. Besides that."

Claire Thornton rubbed her hands together, trying to generate a little heat. She had on thick gloves, thick socks, two sweaters, and a heavy coat. God, she hated the cold. Almost as much as she hated small towns like Denville. Her feelings weren't random. She had grown up in place just like it.

Iowa. Oklahoma. The only difference was the accents. The day they handed her that little high school diploma, she was on the first Greyhound out of town. She didn't look at the destination or ask any questions. As long as it got her far away from where she was, she was willing to take her chances on what she found on the other end.

Turned out what she found was damn good.

"He doesn't appear to be favoring his right leg."

Claire turned to her companion. Three things kept her from punching him in the jaw for dragging her here.

First. She owed him. His faith and support helped her rise so far in a male-dominated business. Second. He had a jaw like granite. She was more likely to hurt herself than him. Third. Gaige Benson had a smile that could charm the angels from heaven. She couldn't stay annoyed when he turned those pearly whites her way.

"No," Claire admitted. "I didn't see a limp. From what you've told me, that's new."

"Last year when Logan reported for training camp, he tried to hide it. It was clear after the first day that his leg was still too weak to hold up to any kind of prolonged physical activity. He ran around this town for over an hour. That has to be a good sign."

"His leg is better, Gaige." Claire sipped her lukewarm coffee. Grimacing, she set the metal travel cup in the holder by her seat. *Keeps things warm for eight hours, my ass.* "We both know there's a huge difference between a leisurely jog and wear and tear of an NFL game."

"We won't know until we try."

Claire shook her head. You couldn't argue with the man. He believed he was always right. The frustrating part? He almost always was. She looked out the window at *Lefty's Pub*. The glow of a faint light shimmered through the tiny window on the door.

Logan Price. Gaige believed there was still something there. It would be Claire's job to find out.

CHAPTER TWO

"MERRY, FUCKING, CHRISTMAS."

It took all of Logan's control not to spit his sip of coffee across his newly polished bar. He didn't expect to be greeted with those words by the first person through the door. Coming from his favorite cocktail waitress, the crude sentiment was doubly surprising.

"Which of Santa's elves crawled up your ass?"

"It certainly wasn't Happy."

"Wasn't he a dwarf?"

"Dwarf. Elf. Who the hell cares? I sure as hell ain't Snow White *or* Mrs. Claus."

The same age as Logan, Rhonda Sykes had been head cheerleader for the Denville Daredevils. Friday nights he ran from end zone to end zone while she cheered him on. They hadn't dated. Partly because they were friends, mostly because Elmer had staked his claim around the seventh grade.

For the next eight years, Rhonda thought that was just fine. The first time he hit her, she forgave him. The second time, she took their baby girl and moved back in with her mother.

Mama convinced Rhonda that a woman's place was with her husband. No matter what. She was five months pregnant with their son when Elmer knocked out Rhonda's front tooth.

Rhonda didn't go to her mother that time. She moved out. For good. She had a high school education and no work experience, but with one child barely walking and another on the way, she needed to make a living. There was no way she could rely on Elmer to help. The courts could tell him he had to pay child support, actually seeing any of that money was another thing altogether.

When Rhonda applied to be a waitress at *Lefty's Pub*, Jonas Price took one look at her swollen belly and hired her on the spot. Not that he let her do much for the next three months. It wasn't until six weeks after she had given birth that Jonas finally let her lift so much as a tray. He had paid her for doing nothing but sitting. He called it her training period. Rhonda called it the kindest thing any human being had ever done for her.

Rummaging through the perpetual mess of half a dozen lipsticks, at least that many packages of chewing gum, a hairbrush, and who knew what else, she pulled out a crumpled piece of paper. The handgun that slid across the bar made Logan grimace. He knew she had a permit. This was Denville. More residents than not packed some sort of firearm.

The bar, though, was supposed to be a no-weapon zone. It said so clearly in big red letters as one entered *Lefty's Pub*. The words were repeated on each wall. By the jukebox. Next to the pool table. In the bathroom – both men's and women's.

The gun his father kept stashed under the ice machine didn't count. Owner's prerogative. In all the years he had run the place, there had never been a reason to use it. Fingers crossed, he never would.

"I've told you about this, Rhonda." Logan picked up the gun. "For tonight, I'll lock it in the office. Tomorrow, leave it home."

"I'm not going around unarmed when my ex-husband carries a freaking arsenal in his truck."

"Is Elmer giving you trouble again?"

The whole town knew about Elmer Pressman's temper. It was the main reason Rhonda walked out on him three years ago. The fact that they both still lived in Denville and shared two kids made it impossible to get away completely. Every now and then, Elmer made it clear he still thought of Rhonda as his. Usually around the time, she started seeing another man.

"Look at this." Rhonda shoved the paper at Logan. "He's claiming the divorce wasn't legal. Can you believe it? Two years I fought that asshole to sign the papers. Now he says he was coerced. *Him*. Can you believe it?"

"Is that even a thing?"

Logan read the paper. It was full of legal jargon used by lawyers to confuse the matter as much as possible. In college, he had taken a course in basic business law. It wasn't a required subject for his business administration degree. However, it seemed prudent to at least have a working idea of what he was looking at when he was required to sign something official. At the time, Logan had sports contracts in mind. He hadn't found a use for it – until now.

The paper from Elmer's lawyer was a convoluted piece of crap. Since anyone Rhonda hired would see through it in a second, the purpose was obvious. The asshole wanted to cause as much aggravation as possible. By the look of things, he got his wish.

"This threat isn't worth the paper it's printed on, Rhonda." Logan handed it back to her. "What did Pug say?"

"Same as you," she said with a shrug.

Stashing her purse underneath the bar, she tied a red apron, *Lefty's Pub* stenciled across the front, around her slender waist.

For all her problems, Rhonda was still as pretty as when she shook her pom-poms around the football sidelines. A nice, shapely figure. Dark brown hair she wore pulled back in a long, sleek tail bounced when she hustled around on a busy Saturday night. Her equally dark eyes were usually filled with warmth and laughter. Especially when she looked at Deputy Stanley Doughtry. *Pug* to everyone who knew him.

Pug had been in love with Rhonda for as long as he could remember. Hell, as long as anyone could remember. Not a man to keep his feelings to himself, he watched with a heavy heart as Rhonda dated, married, and then suffered for her bad judgment.

Finally, after all these years, Rhonda opened her eyes to what had always been right in front of her. She and Pug planned a spring wedding.

"Elmer can't stop you from getting remarried, Rhonda," Logan assured her. "He can be a pain in the ass. He can rant up and down the streets of Denville. Nobody is listening. Even the few friends he has left turn off that particular tune."

"I know." Rhonda sighed. "It never seems to end, that's all."

"It will. You have a good man. Pug is one of the best. Now," Logan reached behind him, bringing back a box spilling over with large sparkly balls and shiny garlands. "Stop cursing Christmas. It's December 3rd. Time to make this old place look the season."

"I really do love this time of year," Rhonda admitted. She held up a silver star. "Especially now that Lacy and Jacob are old enough to really enjoy what's going on."

"Then have at it. I'll be in the office going over the books."

"You don't want to help?"

"I'm more of a look, don't touch, kind of guy when it comes to decorations."

"It's not just the decorations you aren't touching," Rhonda muttered as she started to untangle a string of lights.

"Sorry," Logan looked up from the receipts he had collected from the till. "What were you saying?"

"You need to get laid," Rhonda said frankly. "Don't give me that look. You hurt your leg not your… you know."

"My…?" Logan prompted. "Go on. If you can say laid, you can say… you know."

"Fine." Rhonda pulled her five foot three frame onto a barstool. "From all accounts, you've been living like a monk since you returned to Denville."

"From all accounts." Logan shook his head in amazement. "How the hell does greater Denville know what I do in my own time? I might have a different woman up to my place every night."

"Who would make up this caravan of women?" Rhonda cocked her head to the side. "If you were taking any of the Denville women up on their offers, the whole town would know. The first one who gets you will shout it to the rafters.

"Jesus." Logan rolled his eyes.

"And why not? Despite the mountain look you're currently sporting, there's a damn good-looking man under all that hair. Tall, trim body. All that running you do has kept the gut off. Most of the guys we went to school with can't say that."

"Thanks. I think."

"You aren't importing these phantom sex partners. That would definitely circulate through the morning coffee klatches."

"Okay, Rhonda. I get the point. Can we please drop the subject?"

Rhonda ignored him. "You aren't doing cyber-sex, are you?"

"I give up." Logan stalked toward the office. "Don't bother me unless there's an emergency."

Logan closed the office door.

Christ. When had he become so pathetic that even his lack of a sex life was fodder for the town gossip mill? It was too late to simply pick an unattached woman and sleep with her. After so long, that would cause an even bigger stir.

Logan sighed. It looked like it was either masturbation or nothing. More and more, he was fine with nothing.

Lack of sex drive couldn't be a good thing in an otherwise healthy twenty-seven-year-old male.

Tossing the receipts on the desk, he collapsed onto the old leather chair. When he was a kid, he would roll it from one side of the room to the other, concocting elaborate adventures.

Sometimes he was a pirate, his ship's sails carrying him to exotic foreign shores. Other times, he was a racecar driver, spinning out, and then saving himself at the last minute as he crossed the finish line in victory.

Today it was simply a chair. He wished he could recall even the tiniest bit of the magic and wonder he imbued into it. The days of wishing were over. His imagination was a vast wasteland. Logan Price was firmly grounded in reality. He had been for some time. The sooner he came to grips with that, the better off he would be.

Logan opened the ledger. He was good at numbers. Always had been. One plus two equals three. Simple. Absolute.

Torn-up knee equals the end of a football career. That one was harder to calculate. Unfortunately, for Logan Price, the answer was still set in stone.

CHAPTER THREE

FOR THE FIRST time in weeks, Logan felt like sleep would welcome him instead of mock him.

His eyes felt heavy. His body and mind longed to shut down for a solid eight hours. No tossing. No dreaming. Nothing but blissful, uneventful slumber.

Now all he had to do was clear out the stragglers. Last call had been twenty minutes ago. Time to pack it in.

Logan was just about to roust Rafer and his table when the bar door swung open.

"Sorry," he called out to the man and woman. "We're about to close up."

"It's a damn chilly night. Can't you spare a cup of coffee?"

Son of a bitch. Gaige Benson.

Logan found himself doing something he didn't do very often. Seeing his old QB standing in the middle of *Lefty's Pub*, he grinned.

"Take a seat," Logan said. "I'll be with you in a minute."

"Make sure the coffee is hot. Preferably scalding."

Logan looked at Gaige. The other man shrugged.

"Claire isn't a big fan of cold weather."

"Don't worry, sweetheart," Rafer called out, grabbing his crotch. "I've got a hot meat injection that will warm you right up."

Claire simply rolled her eyes and headed for a table on the other end of the bar.

"Time to clear out." Logan slapped his palm next to the head of Cyrus Lott. He had dozed off on the bar about an hour ago.

"Fuck you, Price." The man's eyes focused for a second on Logan before his head dropped back down.

"Hey," Rafer called out. "Show some respect, Cy. Old Price almost used to be somebody."

Rafer's pals burst out laughing. It was an old jab, but a favorite one.

"You too." Logan stared Rafer down. As usual, the other man blinked first. "Take it someplace else."

Grumbling, the men got to their feet. They took as much time as they could without pushing it. They knew from experience that Logan wasn't adverse to literally kicking their asses out the door.

"Hey," Logan called out. He pointed to Cyrus. "Don't forget this one."

With more grumbling, two of the men grabbed Cyrus under the arms, dragging him out the door.

"Charming group." Rather than wait, Gaige was behind the bar, pouring three cups of coffee. He grabbed a handful of creamers and a couple of spoons. "Are they always so complimentary?"

Turning the closed sign, Logan locked the door. He hit the switch, shutting off the outdoor lights.

"Keeps me humble."

Gaige snorted. "There's humbling, then there's self-flagellation. Going home is one thing, Logan." Gaige looked around. "This is just plain depressing."

"Hey." Logan shot Gaige a warning look. "My dad built this place from nothing. I won't listen to you putting it down."

"I'm not talking about the bar, kid."

Logan winced at the use of his old nickname.

"It's a nice bar. As bars go."

Logan looked at the woman. *Really* looked. What he saw gave his libido a slight tug. Big blue eyes. Full lips. A few strands of blond hair peeked from under the heavy knit cap that she had pulled down over her ears. He couldn't see much of a shape under her black pea coat.

Not that it mattered. The slight tug he felt was just that. Slight. His libido wasn't coming out to play. She could strip down naked and have the body of a goddess. These days his erections were brief and quickly taken care of. Women, even one with lips like that held little interest.

"Logan, this is Claire Thornton."

"I would shake your hand, but that would mean removing one from this mug. Sorry. Not happening."

"It isn't that cold." Logan frowned. "Are you ill?"

"Healthy as a horse." Claire sipped the steaming liquid, sighing with pleasure. "Good coffee."

"I always brew a fresh pot around closing time."

"To sober up your customers?"

Logan couldn't help it. His eyes followed as Claire's lips circled the rim of the cup. A-one lips.

"What do you give the drunks?"

"If I can't find anyone else, a ride home. With their heads out the window. You let one guy spew his guts all over your upholstery, you don't make that mistake again."

"I imagine."

Nice voice, too. Kind of husky.

"The coffee thing is a myth."

"Oh?" Claire's eyes lit up with interest.

"The only thing that sobers up a drunk is time. Throwing up helps a bit. Once the alcohol is in your blood, no amount of caffeine is going to help."

"Are you two finished?"

Well, hell. For a moment, Logan forgot Gaige was there. He was so caught up talking to Claire that... He suddenly had a horrible thought. Were Gaige and Claire a couple? Stupid question. Why else would they be traveling together? He felt a sinking feeling in his stomach. He might not be interested, but for some reason, the idea of Gaige and Claire made him slightly ill.

"How long have you two been seeing each other?"

"See?" Claire looked at Gaige in confusion. Then it hit her. "Oh. *Seeing*."

Claire burst out laughing. To keep from spilling her coffee, she set it down on the table. When Gaige sighed, she almost doubled over.

"It isn't that funny."

"You're right." Claire wiped the moisture from her eyes. "We hit the friend zone the moment we met. Thinking of you any other way struck me as ridiculous."

"There you have it." Gaige gave a self-deprecating laugh. "The story of my life. All the good women want to be friends."

"Boo hoo." Claire picked up her cup. "One supermodel after another. It's a tough life, buddy."

Gaige simply shrugged. His love life was well documented. Fourteen years as a top-tier NFL quarterback came with many perks. It also meant a certain loss of privacy. You would never hear him complain about either. Gaige had loved every second.

"I've been waiting for you to ask me why we've come to see you."

"You mean you weren't just in the neighborhood?" Logan asked with mock surprise. "I've lost track of how many ex-teammates have dropped by in the middle of the season."

"Gotta love the sarcasm." Gaige chuckled.

"I don't want to know, Gaige." Logan slid back his chair. He reached behind the bar, grabbing the half-full pot of coffee. "Refill?"

"Thanks." Claire held out her cup.

"Not for me." Gaige waited until Logan took his seat. "This is our bye week. It's early December and for the second straight year, the Knights are making the playoffs."

"I know," Logan nodded. "Five and eight with three to play. It's rough."

"Brutal." Gaige looked Logan in the eye. "Next year is going to be my last. I'm retiring."

"What?" Logan couldn't believe what he was hearing. "Why? You're still at the top of your game. Healthy. Young."

"Now you're stretching it."

"Okay," Logan conceded. "Youngish. You haven't lost a step. Why walk away?

"I'll be thirty-eight years old next year." *Jesus*, Gaige thought. *Where had the years gone?* "You say I haven't lost a step. I know different. I don't bounce back like I used to. My knees feel more like I'm pushing fifty, instead of forty."

Logan nodded. Knees were tricky. No one knew that better than he did.

"What does all that have to do with me?"

"I have one more chance to grab the brass ring." Gaige leaned closer. "I plan on going out a winner, kid. And you're going to help me."

"How am I supposed to do that?"

"I need you with me next year."

Logan scoffed. "As what? Ball boy."

"Running back."

"You need your head examined." Logan shot out of his chair.

"Nice speed."

"Fuck you." He started pacing. "There's no way I'm going to humiliate myself again. The last time I tried to come back I was *politely* asked to leave after the first week. They'd laugh in my face if I even suggested giving me another chance."

"*They*," Gaige smiled. "Are already onboard."

Logan stopped in his tracks.

"Everyone?"

"Yes."

"Management?"

Gaige nodded.

"Coach Coleman?"

"We can go through the list," Gaige said. "You'd be hard-pressed to find someone who doesn't want to give you another shot."

"Why?" Logan had a hard time wrapping his head around the entire idea.

"You seem to forget, kid. Teams always invite wild cards to training camp. Early days are for looking at all the possibilities."

"Those *possibilities* rarely work out."

"I get that you're scared." Gaige patted the chair. When Logan was seated, he made his big pitch. "Here's the reason the Knights are giving you another look. In the last two years, our running game has been nonexistent. I don't have to tell you that. You've been following the team."

"What makes you say that?" Logan asked casually.

He wasn't ready to admit how he had kept up with the team. On his many sleepless nights, if he wasn't out running, he scoured the internet for every scrap of information. He knew where the Knights needed help. He didn't believe it would come from him.

"You knew our record," Gaige challenged.

"I work in a bar." Logan shrugged. "If a game isn't on the TV, someone is talking about one.

"So everything you know about the Knights you absorbed. Football by osmosis."

Claire gave a short laugh into her cup. Logan's focus shifted to her.

"If you aren't with Gaige as his girlfriend, why are you here?"

"I'm—"

"We'll get to that," Gaige interrupted. He gave Claire a look Logan didn't understand. Apparently Claire did. She simply shrugged and went back to sipping her coffee.

"I have one question." Gaige gave Logan one of his patented unwavering stares. During a game, that look said to the team *trust me; I have your back – no matter what.* It had never failed to send a jolt of confidence through Logan. Now was no exception.

"Shoot."

"Are you happy with all this?" Gaige jerked his head toward the bar. "No shame if you are."

Logan hesitated. He wanted to jump at the chance Gaige dangled in front of him. It wasn't simply about believing in his QB. It was about believing in himself. At one time, that was a no-brainer. Now? His faith was more than a little shaky.

"It's obvious you aren't sleeping. The late-night runs."

"How do you know about that?" Logan demanded. The second he asked the question, the answer came to him.

"Son of a bitch, Gaige. You've been talking to my father."

"He called me, Logan." Gaige put a hand on Logan's shoulder. "Don't be angry. He's worried about you."

"Then all of this?" Logan felt his frustration growing. "Pity, Gaige? My father guilted you into it?"

"Hell, no." Gaige almost shouted the words. "There's no room for sentimentality in pro football. I had already approached Coach Coleman before I spoke with your dad. He simply reinforced what I already suspected. You aren't through with the game, Logan. It's time to find out if the game is really through with you."

Logan scrubbed his hands over his face. For the first time in months, the beard bothered him. Itchy. Pulling on one section, he stretched it out to its full length. Rhonda was right. He *was* starting to resemble a mountain man.

"Goddamn it, Gaige. I don't know whether to hate you or…"

"Finish that after you make the team."

Gaige slapped Logan on the back, his dark brown eyes brimming over with good humor. It was easy to be happy when you knew you'd won. It was a feeling he was used to. Gaige Benson was a winner. First in high school. Then college. As a pro, he had it all – except that elusive championship ring. He planned on going out on top. Pulling Logan up with him would make the win that much sweeter.

"I appreciate your belief in me, Gaige." Logan wished he still possessed half of the QB's confidence. Hell, right now he'd settle for a few drops. "I still don't understand why you think anything has changed. The leg isn't as strong as it used to be. Case closed."

"That's where Claire comes in."

Claire looked at Gaige, her eyebrows raised.

"Oh," she said, her blue eyes wide. "Is it my turn to speak?"

"Keep the sass to a minimum," Gaige warned.

"Sass." Claire slowly rolled the word off her tongue, weighing the meaning. "My daddy called it something else."

Using words not fit for mixed company. Certainly not fit for a thirteen-year-old girl. Then again, her father's vocabulary hadn't exactly been varied. He liked to stick to the four-letter adjectives whenever possible.

"Claire?"

"Right." She nodded at Gaige before turning her attention to Logan. "I'm going to get that leg back to game shape." Claire mentally crossed her fingers. "The rest will be up to you."

"Are you a witch or a miracle worker?" Logan scoffed. "I've been to the best orthopedic specialists money can buy. They told me it is what it is. Time to learn to live with it."

The fact that he even listened to Gaige's idea spoke volumes about how well he was *living with it*.

"There's the difference."

"What's the difference?"

"Money can't buy me."

"Yet," Gaige added.

"Exactly," Claire grinned. She winked at Logan. "Take advantage of me now while my price is rock-bottom cheap."

"You're going to help me out of the goodness of your heart?"

"I love a healthy dose of cynicism." Claire set her cup down. "Call it quid pro quo." She winked at Gaige. "Latin. Bet there was a time you never thought to hear that come out of my mouth."

"True, but I had hope." Gaige beamed. "Look at you now. Little Claire is all grown up."

"I'm sure there's a fascinating story there." Logan sighed with frustration. "For now, can we get back to how you plan to get me back to the NFL?"

"It won't be easy." Claire was suddenly all business. "I've looked at your medical records."

"Aren't those confidential?"

Gaige shrugged. "I know a few people."

"What does it matter? No need to blush." Claire asked. "Yours aren't the first x-rays I've encountered. Trust me, I've seen it all." She leaned closer. "No guarantees, Logan, but I think I can help."

"She's…?" Logan looked at Gaige.

"Arrogant. Cocky."

"Gee, thanks." Claire batted her eyelashes.

"If you're asking for her qualifications?"

"That would be nice," Logan said.

"She has a shiny new Master's degree in sports science."

"With an emphasis on neurobiology and bioenergetics," Claire added conversationally.

Seeing the look of bewilderment on Logan's face, Gaige laughed.

"I have no idea what all that means either. Except," he continued when Logan would have spoken. "Claire knows her way around an athlete."

"Taken out of context, I might find that insulting."

"Might?"

Claire turned her head, giving Logan the once over.

"I do like a man in uniform."

"Forget her fresh mouth, Logan." Gaige sent Claire another warning look. "The point is, Claire knows her stuff."

"Who have you worked with?"

"You'll be it," Claire said. "Hey, you should be honored. They say a girl never forgets her first."

"Really?" Logan focused on Gaige. He couldn't decide if Claire was the most interesting woman he had ever met or the most exasperating.

"You'll never be bored," Gaige assured him with a shrug.

Boredom was increasingly his enemy. It ranked right up there with depression, mixed with a big dose of self-pity. He was sick of it all. Mostly, he was sick of himself. Gaige threw him a lifeline in Claire. She looked at him with her killer blue eyes waiting for his decision. She was smart with a quick wit and a smart mouth. Damn. That mouth might get them both in trouble.

"You really know what you're doing?"

Claire put down her cup. Standing, she held out her hand. When Logan took it in his, she gave it a shake, her grip surprisingly strong.

"I believe in myself, Logan. I've had to. If you put your faith in me, I won't let you down."

Logan didn't know how he felt about all of this. It was too new – too unexpected. Gaige believed in Claire. Logan believed in Gaige. For now, it was enough.

"Tell me how this is going to work.

CHAPTER FOUR

LOGAN SHOULD HAVE known Gaige would have a plan in place. The man was a field general of the highest caliber. You didn't last for so many years in the pressure cooker that was the NFL without coming to the game fully prepared and ready for battle.

"You have two choices," Gaige told him. "Announce to the world you're trying for a comeback."

"Hell, no."

Gaige held up a hand. "Hear me out. If you make it public, you'll garner a lot of sympathy. We might even get ESPN down here to do an hour-long profile."

"And when I fall flat on my face, the ending will be a few lines written over the screen about failed dreams or some kind of crap like that."

"*If* you fail. But I get what you're saying." Gaige sat back in his chair. "Choice number two. No press. No announcements. Fly under the radar until the last possible moment."

"I'll move here for the next six months," Claire jumped in. "As far as anyone will know, I'm an old girlfriend. We reconnected online. I decided to move in with you so we could pick up where we left off."

"Just like that."

"Are you implying that I couldn't talk you into such an arrangement?"

"I'm stating flat out that you'd be an idiot to want anything to do with me." Logan shook his head in amazement. "Who is going to buy that a woman like you would drop everything to live here? With me?"

"Is he saying I'm too good for him?" Claire asked Gaige.

"That's how it sounded."

"Well, then." She grinned. "I won't argue the point. We make it look good; why should anyone care?"

"What constitutes good?" Logan was fascinated in spite of himself.

"Hand holding. Brief kisses. Little touches." Claire shrugged. "We don't have to rip each other's clothes off."

"You just have to look like you want to." Gaige finished for her.

"Exactly."

Logan let the idea sink in. He'd meant what he said. There was nothing in Denville for a woman like Claire. Not on a personal level. She was beautiful. Educated. Everything was in front of her.

Logan had one thin chance at the future he'd always dreamed of having.

Looking at Claire's vibrant face, he felt that stirring of attraction again. Now wasn't the time for his libido to come out of hibernation. He would be better off if it stayed where it was for the next six months. Fail or succeed, he could worry about his sex life when all of this was settled.

"Well? What will it be?" Claire placed her hand over his. "Am I your faux-girlfriend or not?"

Claire's touch sent a jolt through his body. *Down, boy,* Logan admonished his dick. *Don't blow it for us now.*

"We need a new place to live, *sweetheart*. My place would send you screaming all the way back to Seattle."

AS IT TURNED out, Claire didn't scream. Compared to her childhood home, Logan's one room over his father's garage resembled a four-star hotel.

It was clean. There were no odd smells that you were better off not identifying – not if she wanted to sleep nightmare-free. A bed with a new mattress? Hot running water?

Logan didn't know how good he had it. He should try sharing a bedroom the size of his average closet with his older sisters. Rather than cram herself into the middle, she slept on the floor more often than not.

The year before Claire left home, her oldest sister ran away with the first guy who asked. It cleared half the bed. However, eleven months of relative comfort didn't keep Claire from hopping on that Greyhound.

"It's not that bad." She bounced a couple of times on the mattress.

"Any particular reason you're staying out here instead of in that big old house with your dad?"

"Privacy?"

"For all those women you aren't bringing home at night?"

"How did you —"

"I didn't," Claire laughed. "It was a guess which you just confirmed."

Frowning, Logan watched as Claire circled the small room. She stopped to run a finger over the counter in the kitchenette. Seeming satisfied, she opened the two-burner oven.

"Is this place clean because you never use it, or are you a Felix?"

"I don't cook," Logan muttered. "Wait. Am I a what?"'

"A Felix." Claire was bent over examining the almost empty mini-fridge. "You know. As in *The Odd Couple*? Felix was the clean one, Oscar the slob."

Christ, TV references.

"I never watched much television." Except football. He devoured as many of those as possible.

"I did." Claire practically beamed with pride. "We got an old secondhand black and white when I was seven. Two channels – on a good night. The antenna picked up more static than anything else but when it worked, it was glorious."

"It didn't take much to entertain you."

Claire laughed. It was such a happy sound. Happy had been in short supply in his life for some time. Like a starving man presented with a crumb, Logan wanted more.

Searching his mind, he tried to think of something that would have her filling the room with that joyous sound. He used to know a few jokes, though not ones you told in mixed company.

"What has you looking so intense?"

With a start, Logan realized Claire was standing in front of him. *When had she crossed the room?* And why did she have to smell so good?

"I was wondering if I could make you laugh again." No reason to lie. "I like the way it sounds."

"You should kiss me."

Claire said it in such a matter of fact way, Logan was sure he misunderstood."

"Kiss you?"

"It's obvious we have a mutual attraction going here," Claire said. She moved a step closer.

"Mutual?"

"As in you're interested." Putting a hand on his shoulder, Claire tilted her head. "As in, despite the whole Grizzly Adams routine, I'm feeling that little flutter in my stomach."

When Logan didn't respond, Claire raised an eyebrow. "Don't tell me you've never heard of Grizzly Adams?"

"I have an inkling."

Knowing it was a bad idea, Logan circled Claire's waist with his hands. Slender. No longer wearing that bulky winter coat, her figure was nicely displayed by a pair of faded jeans and an impossibly soft sweater only slightly darker in color than her eyes. She was average height, the slight heel on her leather boots bringing her to just under his chin.

Her shoulder-length hair looked like golden sunlight and bounced when she walked. Logan wanted to slide his fingers into the thick locks. He would take what she offered. A long, deep, hot kiss. Then… What? As tempting as it sounded, he knew a bad idea when he heard one.

"I'm not hitting on you."

"Has that kind of thing changed in the year and a half that I've been cut off from civilization?"

Claire laughed. Damn. Logan unconsciously moved closer. Honey. That's what it sounded like. And he was a very horny bee.

"I can control my urges," she assured him.

"Me too." *Probably.*

"It's wondering that always gets me in trouble. I don't want to spend the next six months wondering what your kiss is like." Claire moved her mouth to a hair's breadth from his. "Once I know, I can put it out of my mind."

Logan could have stopped her. The problem was he didn't want to. The second her lips brushed across his, there was no turning back. He had to know what she tasted like.

Gripping her waist, Logan kept their bodies from touching. If this was going to stop at a kiss, he wasn't taking any chances. If her sweet curves started rubbing against him, there would be no turning back.

"For this to work, you need to participate."

As Claire said the words, she bit his lower lip. Hard.

"Hey," Logan protested.

"I needed you to open up. Thank you."

Her tongue slid in, challenging his to keep up. With a growl and a curse, Logan opened a little more. Claire wanted a kiss? Then that was what she would get.

Logan slanted his mouth over Claire's, his tongue rubbing sensuously over hers. It might have been awhile, but he remembered exactly how to make a woman lose control. Not too hard. Just soft enough. Long. Slow. Deep. Wet. It was an art. Once, he was a master. Like playing an instrument, it wasn't long until he hit all the right notes.

Claire didn't pull away when the kiss ended. She slowly backed up, her eyes closed. Slightly parted, her mouth glistened. Taking a deep breath, her lids slowly opened.

"Was that a bad idea?"

"I'm not complaining." For the first time in over a year, Logan felt like his feet were on solid ground. Claire's kiss. Was it that simple?

"Sex would be a mistake, Logan." Claire moved farther away. "Unprofessional. Gaige…"

"If this happens, Gaige will have nothing to do with it," Logan interrupted. His voice was sharp with annoyance.

"Thanks for the *if it happens*." Claire pushed her hair back, a small smile on her lips. "I appreciate that there's no automatic assumption that we will have sex."

"I never assume a woman will drop into my bed, Claire."

Or that if she did, he would be able to do anything about it. Logan's dick showed signs of life, thanks to Claire. It would be humiliating to have it die on him at the wrong moment. He wanted to be sure that all his parts worked before things got that far. If he found himself needing those little blue pills to perform? Hell, shoot him now. His misery would be complete.

"There's always Viagra."

"What?" Logan barked in surprise. Witch, miracle worker, and mind reader? Having Claire Thornton around would be continually disconcerting if she kept this up.

"You zoned out." Claire tapped his temple. "I was telling you about the guy in my deep tissue massage class. Students would practice on students. Sometimes instructors."

"One of them took Viagra before your massage?"

"Not with me in mind," Claire said. "Not at first."

"Was this a legitimate class or something you signed up for in the back of a magazine? You know. The kind with large-breasted women on the cover?"

"I don't read *Jugs*."

"How do you know that's the one I meant?" Logan gave Claire an innocent smile. "Maybe I was referring to *Vogue*."

"According to Vogue, big-breasted women don't exist. It ruins the line of those designer clothes."

"I like breasts."

"What man doesn't?" Claire laughed. "My massage instructor was a big fan."

"What happened?" Logan offered Claire a seat before sitting in the only other chair in the room.

"Seems he planned on meeting his girlfriend right after class. In anticipation, he took some Viagra. He figured a little stimulation from me, some chemical enhancement, and boom – he'd be ready to screw the night away."

"I take it the pills took effect a little earlier than planned?"

Claire nodded. "I worked my magic on his back. When I asked him to turn over, tent city."

Logan snickered.

"Why?" Claire joined in, laughing and shaking her head. "He could have stayed on his stomach. Instead, he proudly yanked off the sheet yelling *ta da*. There were four other students in the room. Luckily one of them was a woman."

"The guys weren't any help?" Suddenly the story didn't seem as funny. The situation could have turned ugly. Fast.

"They were too busy laughing their asses off. June and I hightailed it out of there. We stopped just long enough to report what happened."

"Did the instructor lose his job?"

"Nope."

"What?"

"He was given a warning." Claire sighed. "I was eighteen. Working two jobs while I took classes at a community college just outside of Tacoma. Every cent I could scrape together went toward my education."

"You should have sued the bastard. And the college."

"I didn't have the time or any backup. June didn't want to get involved. The two male students said they didn't see anything. It came down to he said, she said. In the end, I got my money back. I had to settle for that."

Logan imagined it was harder than she was making out. A young woman on her own, even one as capable and strong-willed as Claire would always be a target for men who wanted to take advantage of her.

"So how did you get from there to here? Where does Gaige enter the picture?"

"That's an even longer story."

"It's five o'clock in the morning. Unless you want to go for a run, there isn't much else to do in Denville."

"Give me five minutes." Claire grabbed her bag.

She'd only brought the one in case Logan rejected Gaige's proposal. It would do for a week or so. Once she had Logan on a regular routine, she would take a day to fly back to Seattle. There were things she needed now that she knew where she would be for the next six months.

"You want to go running?" Logan watched as Claire pulled several things from her duffle.

"I can talk and run." She paused at the bathroom door. "Can't you?"

"It's never come up," he mumbled to the closed door.

Solitary. That was what his life had become. Work and home. He ate with his dad a couple times a week. They shared a beer now and then. Until Gaige mentioned his father calling, Logan had no idea how much worry he caused him.

Jonas Price wasn't a talkative man. He rarely shared his feelings. The happiest he could ever remember seeing his father was on the day the Knights drafted Logan. Jonas bought a round for the house. Beaming, he toasted his son on the beginning of a long and successful career.

That image stayed with Logan. Through training camp. Making the team. His first touchdown. Waking up in the hospital after surgery on his fractured leg. The realization his career was over. It made it that much harder to come home a failure.

Logan went through the familiar motions of pulling on his running clothes, his mind occupied with thoughts of his father. It couldn't have been easy. The comments Logan endured were one thing. Knowing some of that had to have spilled over onto his father ripped at his guts.

Hard working. Honest. Jonas Price never asked for help. Not for himself. Calling Gaige Benson would have been difficult for such a proud man. He loved his son. Logan never doubted it. He would swallow his pride if it meant helping his only child.

"Ready?"

Claire was dressed all in black. Shoes, snug Lycra pants, and a thick zippered jacket. Her gloves and knit cap with all her hair tucked inside made her look like a cat burglar, not a physical therapist.

"What?" Claire demanded, looking up as she re-tied her left shoe.

"Fancy gear."

Claire gave him the once over. "You need better shoes. Those don't give you the proper support. How long have you had them? There are holes on top of the holes."

"I found them in the closet of my old room." Logan turned his foot to the side, examining the old shoe. "They serve their purpose."

"Crack open the wallet, Logan." Claire zipped her jacket up to her chin. "Your feet will thank you."

As they headed down the outside stairs, Logan glanced over at the house where he grew up. Old, rambling, neat as a pin. His father wouldn't have had it any other way. Even when money was at its tightest, Jonas Price never let their home be rundown. What he couldn't take care of himself, he would barter to get it done. Services for services. From a new coat of paint to roof repair. Jonas always found a way.

Logan set off in his usual direction with Claire by his side. The house was as dark as the rest of the town. In a few hours, his father would be up, having his morning coffee. Checking the sports headlines on ESPN. Football. It got Jonas' juices flowing. Seeing his son's name in print once again would mean the world to a man who asked for little.

Up until this moment, he hadn't been sold that this was a good idea. Now, picking up the pace, he was determined to make it work.

I won't let you down again, Dad.

THEY RAN IN silence. One mile, then two. If Claire was anything like him, her brain worked harder than her body. A million thoughts ricocheting off each other at the speed of light.

Gaige left Denville over an hour ago. He had a plane to catch so he could get back to Seattle for a workout with his personal trainer.

The Knights season might be a lost cause, but Gaige wouldn't slack. Every game, no matter the team's record, was played with the intensity of the playoffs.

Before he left, they nailed down the details of the plan.

"Finding a place for you and Claire to work out on the QT presented the biggest problem. Your dad took care of that. He volunteered his basement."

"Jesus, Gaige." Logan couldn't believe what he was hearing. "How long has this been in the works? Without my knowledge."

"About a month."

Logan let out a long string of expletives. Gaige patiently waited for him to finish. Claire calmly continued sipping her coffee.

"Getting workmen in and out was no problem," Gaige continued matter-of-factly. "He told his neighbors he was doing a little remodeling."

"Remodeling? In Denville?" Amazed, Logan shook his head.

"All I can tell you is it worked. The job was finished two days ago."

"And I didn't notice a thing."

"That's what happens when you get so wrapped up in your own crap. The world tends to pass you by."

Knowing Claire had it right didn't make her words any easier to take. Ignoring her, Logan turned to Gaige.

"How much is all this costing you?"

"No." Gaige shook his head. His dark green eyes bit into Logan like shards of steel. "This isn't about that. You're a friend, Logan. Money can't be an issue. Not now."

"Gaige…"

"Don't even think about paying me back. Someday, when the opportunity presents itself, pay it forward."

In other words, give someone a hand up. Logan agreed with the sentiment. It rankled knowing he couldn't do anything about it now. He had holed himself away, wallowing in self-pity. He had a degree. There was nothing stopping him from using it.

Nothing except his own stubborn pride. To get a job that paid a decent wage, he would have to use his waning celebrity. He would be a poster boy in a suit. His bosses could trot him out to shake hands and polish the company image. The likelihood that he would ever do any actual work was slim to none.

Logan wasn't looking for an easy paycheck.

That's why he would work his ass off for this second chance. If and when he made the big bucks, it would be because he earned it. Then, when he saw somebody floundering, he would follow Gaige's directive. He would pay it forward.

"Ready to talk?"

Logan glanced at Claire. A fine sheen of perspiration covered her forehead, but she breathed normally. She kept pace with ease even though his stride was longer. This woman was in shape. Add one more thing to her sexy column.

"Nothing was keeping you quiet," Logan pointed out. "Not that anything could."

"I do like to speak my mind." Claire wasn't offended. "It seemed you needed to sort a few things out. I thought I would give you a few miles to organize your thoughts."

"Thanks." Logan slowed his pace. "I do have a few questions."

"Only a few?" Claire turned. Running backward, she looked Logan in the eye. "I'll take as many as you've got."

"Even the personal ones?"

"Sure." Claire shrugged. "I can't guarantee I'll answer."

"Fair enough. Tell me how you met Gaige."

"No problem there." Clair fell back in step. "I love that story."

After she left her class at the community college, Claire added a third job to her day. If she wasn't learning, she would be earning. In a few months when classes started up again, she had planned to have a nice little nest egg accumulated.

The waitress job at *Chuck's Pancake House* didn't pay much, but the tips made up for it. It turned out truckers liked a pretty girl who didn't mind partaking in a little mild flirtation while serving them.

Her shift was the early one. Five a.m. to noon. Most of the men needed a break and a hot meal. They didn't have time for more than a smile and some friendly conversation. The few times anyone got fresh, she had a dozen or so burly protectors watching her back.

Claire had worked at *Chuck's* for over a month when Gaige Benson and three other Knights walked into the restaurant. She didn't recognize them, but everyone else did.

"You think that's funny?" Claire swerved into Logan, knocking off his stride. She sped up, making him pick up his pace to catch her.

"You were saying?"

Claire shot him a smile. You had to love a guy who didn't mind a woman getting the better of him.

"Even though it was a slow part of the morning, Gaige, and his crew caused quite a stir."

Claire used the lull to refill salt and pepper shakers. If she got it done now, she could cut out a little early. She had a new book on human musculature that she was dying to crack open.

"That's Gaige Benson," Susie Wade whispered.

Having just arrived for the next shift, Susie was still taking off her coat.

"That's nice."

Claire's concentration was on not spilling salt all over the place. She didn't know who Gaige Benson was and she didn't care. Men were such a low priority in her life right now; they might as well not exist.

"Nice is putting it mildly." Susie sighed. "I don't know the other two guys. Al says they play with the Knights, too."

Finished, Claire screwed on the last shaker cap. She glanced at the clock. Ten minutes and she was out of here.

"OMG." Susie grabbed Claire's arms, almost sending the tray of salt and pepper flying.

"Careful, Susie." She liked the other woman, but sometimes she could be a pain in Claire's ass.

"He's sitting in your station. Damn. Ten more minutes and he would have been mine."

"Hey, knock yourself out."

Claire was more than happy to turn what's his name over to the other waitress. Maybe she would get out of here early after all.

"That's your table, Claire." Chuck leaned through the kitchen door. "You're still on the clock, aren't you?"

"Sorry, Susie."

Making sure her pad and pen were in her apron pocket. Damn, Chuck. He was a good boss. Fair. However, he was a stickler for working her full shift. Sometimes, when he wasn't looking, Claire snuck away a few minutes early. No such luck today.

She approached the table with her usual friendly smile. Fact. Happy waitresses got better tips. Claire wasn't going to let a minor disappointment cost her even a few dollars. Not when every one was so precious.

"Good morning, gentlemen." She set three glasses of water on the table. "Can I start you with something to drink? Coffee? Juice?"

"Now aren't you a ray of sunshine on a gloomy Seattle day?"

Great. Why was there always one who thought he was a charmer? Claire didn't let her smile slip. She was tired. Her feet hurt. All she wanted was her tiny apartment and her anatomy book. Instead, she was stuck with three…What had Susie called them? Knights? Football. Too bad. She was baseball all the way.

"Should I be insulted?

Logan enjoyed the story. Especially finding she hadn't recognized Gaige. That never happened. This would have been six or seven years ago if he judged properly. Before Logan knew him. Watching his friend's reaction to an oblivious woman was something he was sorry he missed.

"I'm a football convert," Claire assured him. "Though baseball will always be my first love. Before I met Gaige, I planned on becoming the first head trainer for the Mariners."

"Now you plan on getting that job with the Knights?"

"Eventually. Let's take a break."

They were by Newberry Park. A grand name for a place that sported two trees, a single swing, and a bench. Logan never knew who Newberry was or why this little patch of Denville was named after him.

He followed Claire to one of the old oaks. They sat with their backs against the peeling bark. After a minute or so, she picked up her story.

"You're my audition." She rolled her shoulders, breathing in the early morning air. "When I get you back to playing form, I'll be a shoe-in for the assistant trainer job. In the off-season, I'll work toward my PhD. By the time Wally Compton is ready to retire, I can just slide right into the head trainer job."

Impressive. Logan admired ambition and Claire brimmed with it. One more person counting on him. Rather than feeling the weight of expectation, he felt a surge of hope. Why shouldn't they both get what they wanted? She believed it was possible. More and more, so did he.

"Gaige encouraged you?"

"More than that," Claire told him. "He paid for the whole thing."

The first thing Claire noticed about Gaige Benson was his smile. Warm and inviting without a touch of smarm. He shut down his friend with one look. She took their order, served the meal, and cleared the plates. All business. No problems.

When his teammates left, Gaige asked Claire to join him. Thinking she had read him wrong, Claire couldn't help her feeling of disappointment. The nice guy was going to turn out to be the big bad wolf.

"All I want to do is talk," Gaige said, somehow reading her mind. "I promise."

Still leery, Claire took the seat across from one of the most recognizable men in the country.

"Hi," Gaige held out his hand. "My name is Gaige Benson and I play football for the Seattle Knights."

Laughing, Claire shook his hand. "Hi. My name is Claire Thornton and I'm a waitress."

"Pleased to meet you, Claire." Gaige leveled his gaze, capturing hers. "Tell me your dreams."

It was a ridiculous thing to ask of a stranger. Yet for some reason, Claire found herself telling him everything. Three hours later, Claire couldn't believe the turn her life had taken.

"Gaige listened," Claire said. "I don't think anyone had ever done that."

"I know." Closing his eyes, Logan nodded. "Gaige has that rare ability to concentrate his attention on one person. He makes you feel like you're the most interesting person in the room. That's why his team would walk through fire for him."

"I sat down to talk to him, convinced he was after something. When we were through, I agreed to let him pay for my education. Just like that. I don't know how it happened."

"Let me guess," Logan laughed. "He refused to let you pay him back."

Claire nodded. "He suggested I volunteer when I had some free time. Giving back to the community would be all the payment he wanted."

"Sounds like Gaige."

"He wanted to pay my room and board." Claire remembered that argument like it was yesterday. For once, Gaige didn't win. "I would have felt too much like a kept woman. Now that I didn't have to worry about the cost of school, I dropped two of my jobs. Seven years later, here we are."

"Mmm."

The lack of sleep caught up to Logan. Add to it the nerves, excitement, and general terror of Gaige's offer, the adrenaline that had kept him going wore off. The thought of jogging all the way home was more exhausting than the actual act. Half asleep, Logan reached for Claire's hand.

"I'd start calling him Saint Gaige if I hadn't witnessed firsthand how debauched my old friend can be."

"Debauched?" Claire had to hear this. "Tell me every—"

It seemed that was a story for another time. Logan was sound asleep, his head tipped back against the tree, his hand still in hers.

Poor baby. Even with the beard, with his face relaxed in slumber, he looked young. Carefree. Not at all like the wound-up mess that she met a few hours ago.

The hood of his sweatshirt hung low on Logan's forehead, a wisp of dark brown hair peeking out. Unable to help herself, Claire smoothed it back, her hand moving down to gently cup his cheek. She wasn't a beard fan. Still, Logan's was surprisingly soft. When they kissed, the ends caressed her skin instead of irritating it. It added a layer of sensation to an already volatile situation.

Kissing Logan Price had been a bad idea. Why then was she obsessed with doing it again?

"You are trouble with a capital T."

"Funny, I was thinking the same thing about you."

Claire would have pulled away, but Logan trapped her hand against his face.

"What do you think?" he asked. He rubbed her palm along his jaw.

Claire looked into Logan's slightly bloodshot eyes. If she was going to get into trouble, she might as well jump in with both feet.

"Not bad." Leaning closer, she whispered, "I'll bet there's quite a face under all this fur."

Logan chuckled ruefully. "There used to be. I haven't seen it for almost a year. God knows what it looks like."

"If you decide you want to find out, let me know. I used to shave my dad. Not a single nick."

"I'll keep that in mind."

Logan wrapped his hand around Claire's neck, gently tugging her the last few inches until her mouth pressed against his.

"Bad idea?" He gave her a final out.

"We both know it is."

Claire licked his bottom lip. The groan that rushed from his throat was all the incentive she needed. Given a choice between sensible and bad, she picked bad.

Logan took her mouth with a swift confidence he hadn't felt for some time. Her taste was addictive and he couldn't get enough.

"Open for me," he urged. "Let me in."

More than happy to oblige, Claire met Logan's tongue halfway. The slip and slide made her squirm. The heat rushing through her body was both thrilling and frustrating. She wanted more. Her instinct was to pull his clothes from his body. How would he feel, naked, hot – hers?

"This isn't the place."

Claire pushed away. There was something to be said for good judgment. Even when it left her body aching. With one last hard, fast kiss, she got to her feet. Holding out her hand, she pulled Logan up.

"Looks like we've moved past if," he said, brushing the dirt from his clothes. "I will have you, Claire."

His words sent a shiver of desire down her spine. Inevitable? Claire had never been a fatalist. She firmly believed in the power of free will. She wanted Logan. Having him was still her choice.

Ready to tell him just that, Claire raised her eyes to Logan's. What she saw made her insides melt. Mixed with need she saw the vulnerability. A proud man whose confidence had eroded to almost nothing. He wasn't demanding her capitulation. He was asking her to take him. Flaws and all. Ride this out to wherever it might lead them.

It was then that Claire knew what Logan needed, but couldn't ask for. Her strength. She would spend the next six months building him up. Inside *and* out. Mind and body.

Claire felt an odd constriction around her heart. This was no longer simply about the job. She cared about Logan. How deeply, time would tell.

"I want you to understand, Logan." Claire pulled his hood over his head. "I don't offer sex in my job description. When we sleep together. And yes, I said when. It won't be for any other reason than I want you."

"I wouldn't have it any other way."

Suddenly energized, Logan took off toward home. Looking over his shoulder, he called out, "What are you waiting for? We only have six months. Let's get to work."

Shaking her head, Claire quickly caught up.

Six months. Half a year spending every day of it with Logan. There it was again. That funny feeling around her heart. Whatever it meant she knew one thing. There was no turning back now.

CHAPTER FIVE

"HOW DID IT go?"

"Good. I think."

Claire closed the door behind her. Sweaty from the run and bone tired from a day of travel, she was ready for a shower and a solid eight hours of sleep. The nap she took on the plane trip from Seattle had worn off long ago.

She smiled with gratitude when Jonas handed her a fresh cup of coffee.

"How did you know I liked it black?"

"Gaige."

Naturally. Claire pulled out a chair at the kitchen table. Her shower could wait a few minutes while she caught up Logan's father.

"Would you like something to eat? Pancakes? Eggs? Toast? Name it."

"I'm not much of a breakfast person. Unless it's for dinner." Claire patted the chair next to her. "Sit. I won't feel comfortable staying here unless you treat me like a friend, not a guest."

"I like to feed my friends." Bringing his cup, Jonas joined her. "We'll get each other's rhythm soon enough."

Claire smiled at the older man. She could see a lot of Logan in him. The same powerful build. His dark hair was liberally sprinkled with gray, but the deep, rich brown was still visible. The eyes got her. The color of rich caramel – exactly like Logan's. He was a handsome man. What made him irresistible was his love for his son. Not all fathers cared that much. Some, like Claire's, couldn't have cared less.

"I like your kitchen. It's homey."

Jonas chuckled, the lines near his eyes a testament that it was something he often did. "Is that your nice way of saying old-fashioned?"

"Nothing wrong with that. New and sleek is fine. So is this."

Claire meant her words. *Architectural Digest* would call it something fancy like Country Chic. She called it welcoming – lived in. Loved.

The white cabinets with copper hardware gleamed. As did the wood block counters and gray tile floor. A stove and refrigerator that, if bought new would be called retro, sparkled as if they had been purchased yesterday instead of when the house was built by Logan's grandfather almost seventy-five years ago. Jonas Price took pride in his home, keeping it well tended – inside and out.

"I know that Gaige called you before he flew back to Seattle." Claire sighed when she tasted the superior coffee. Who said the Pacific Northwest had a premium on the stuff. So far, she loved what Oklahoma had to offer.

Jonas nodded. "Seems Logan wasn't as hard a nut to crack as I thought. Much to my relief."

"He's on board," Claire confirmed. "Not that it means everything will be smooth sailing. Before we're done, Logan will be cursing the day he ever laid eyes on me." Claire lowered her voice conspiratorially. "I'll be pushing him harder than he's ever been pushed."

"Hmm."

"Doubts, Jonas?"

"I'm sure you're very good. It's just—"

"The whole woman thing has you thrown, doesn't it?"

Jonas wasn't the first, or the last, to wonder if a woman belonged in any aspect of men's football. Professional or otherwise. Claire didn't let it bother her. She knew she had what it took. Skill, a bit of a magic touch, and skin like a rhinoceros. She wasn't impervious. However, at this point in her life, it took a hell of a lot to wind up her feelings.

"Give me your hand."

With a touch of hesitation, Jonas did as she asked. Claire noticed the way his fingers were slightly stiff. The way he poured the coffee. How he couldn't quite grip the handle on the cup. Arthritis, if she didn't miss her guess. She couldn't cure it, but she could ease the stiffness and pain.

As she worked each finger with her own, Claire told Jonas about her meeting with Logan. She went over the last few hours. What they talked about. Their long run. The two kisses she left out. That was something best kept private. She moved from first his right hand then to his left, keeping the conversation going while she slowly straightened each finger with a deep, gentle massage. Satisfied with her work, she sat back.

"As I told Logan, there are no guarantees. I'm hopeful, though. From what I've seen, his chances are damn good."

"What did you do?" Jonas flexed his fingers. He couldn't remember the last time he had this much mobility. Or so little pain. In fact, the pain was completely gone. "I've tried every cream on the market. My doctor told me I would have to live with it."

"Your doctor is right. Your arthritis isn't going anywhere." Claire went to the sink. She poured out the last bit before putting her cup in the dishwasher. "What you don't have to live with is the pain and stiffness."

"It's miraculous."

Delighted, Jonas flexed his fingers like a pianist warming up for a recital.

"No," Claire assured him. "If it were a miracle, it would work on everyone. My eye told me your fingers would benefit from my technique."

"How long will it last?"

"Depends. Each person is different." She patted the delighted man on the shoulder. "If you'd like, I'll show you what I did. It's easy when you know the secret."

"I have a feeling you're going to be good for my son *and* me, Claire." Jonas toasted her with his coffee.

With a smile, Claire took the stairs two at a time. Staying in the big house with Jonas made sense. The garage apartment was barely big enough for Logan. Besides, it wasn't anyone's business if they shared a bed. For now, these sleeping arrangements suited Claire. She liked sleeping alone. She loved having her own bathroom. After spending the first eighteen years with neither, they were luxuries she would never take for granted.

Like the kitchen, the bathroom had been designed in a different era. The claw-foot tub was tempting, but Claire was more interested in the big four-poster bed in the other room. After a quick shower, she slathered her body with her one indulgence. Her citrus-scented body lotion. She didn't mind generic toilet paper or bargain basement underwear. When it came to her skin, she didn't skimp. If buying a jar meant skipping lunch for a week, so be it. She inhabited a mostly masculine world. Something that made her feel feminine was worth the occasional empty stomach.

The bedroom was wonderfully warm. Claire appreciated Jonas' thoughtfulness. Not bothering to put anything on, she slipped beneath the soft cotton sheets and downy quilt. Her last thought before she drifted off was of Logan. Hoping he was getting some sleep, she snuggled a little deeper.

Five, six hours at the most. Then they would start their journey. With hard work and a little luck, it would take them all the way. To Seattle. To training camp. To the NFL. And if Gaige had his way – the Super Bowl.

Don't get ahead of yourself, her hazy mind warned. *One step at a time*. She would keep telling herself that. It would be her mantra with Logan.

Still, Claire smiled; it didn't hurt to dream. Which was exactly what she did. In it, she saw Logan, legs strong, going in for the winning touchdown. On the sidelines, she cheered.

No one had to know her private thoughts. Besides, if she was going to dream, why not dream big?

CHAPTER SIX

THE ONLY SOUNDS in the room were the clanking of weights mingling with loud grunts. For the last twenty minutes, Claire had run Logan through a series of progressively intense routines designed to scope out his fitness level.

Claire already knew Logan could run for hours. It turned out that was all he did. To get back in playing shape, he needed increased strength, flexibility, and quickness. From what she had been able to determine, they had a long way to go on all three levels.

The workout room was first rate – no complaints there. The basement of the Price home was spacious. Before Gaige's people got hold of it, Jonas used it for laundry and storage. Now, the washer and dryer were in their own small room off this larger one.

Free weights were lined up against the far wall. Mats, resistance bands in varying color to denote the amount of tension. Towels, a small refrigerator with sports drinks and water. Near the top-of-the-line massage table was a row of cabinets for Claire to store her personal items. Homemade concoctions. Oils, lotions, tonics.

Right now, she ran Logan through the circuit of weight machines that would make any gym-rat drool. Nearing the end of Claire's planned reps and Logan's endurance, she decided to see if she could push a little more. And if he could take it.

"Are you trying to kill me?" Logan huffed out the words, barely able to get his breath.

"You've discovered my evil plot. Find a has-been football player, torture him, and watch as he dies a slow, horrible death. Gaige is in on it, too."

"Urrr."

Logan swallowed the curse words he wanted to spew at Claire. He knew she was his trainer. He should look at her like anyone else doing the job. When he looked at her, however, he saw a woman. A beautiful, desirable woman. His father raised him according to certain rules. He simply didn't use foul language in front of the fairer sex. No matter how much of a sadist she was.

"Go ahead," Claire taunted. "Let it out. It isn't healthy to hold words like that in." She leaned down next to his red, sweating face. "Another thirty seconds and your brain is going to explode."

"Arg."

"You want to be a football player, not a pirate."

Claire kept the smile off her lips and out of her voice. This was day one. She needed Logan to understand who was in charge. Yes, he could bitch, gripe, and generally tell her where to get off. She wanted that. When he started to think of her as his trainer – not a woman – they could really get down to work.

"Give me another set of ten."

Taking a deep breath, Logan gripped the bar. Lat pulls had never been his favorite. Now, he hated them with a passion. With every rep, Claire counted along. Six. Only four more. Seven, eight. *Nine.* Ten was such agony that he finally snapped. As he slowly pulled, he let a long string of curse words in colorful combinations.

"There you go." Claire beamed like a proud parent.

Breathing hard, Logan's chin rested on his heaving chest. He was soaked in sweat. His hands ached from gripping the bar. Tomorrow, his arms and shoulders would be a mass of aches and pains. He couldn't bring himself to worry about a few, or maybe a dozen, expletives.

"In a few hours, I won't be able to move."

Logan took the towel and water bottle that appeared in front of his face. Simultaneously, he wiped his face and drained every last drop of liquid.

"Here." Claire handed him another full bottle. "One more. Then I want you to strip and hop up on the table. You need to hydrate. I need to give you a rubdown. If you start to feel the least bit of stiffness, I'm not doing my job properly."

Logan wasn't so tired he missed the word strip. As in naked. As in naked with Claire's hand on his body. Suddenly *stiff* took on a completely new meaning.

"Maybe I should keep my shorts on."

"Don't be such a guy."

Claire set out a tray of bottles. Each was filled with her own massage oil concoctions. One couldn't find them on the market. *Someday.* Another dream for another time.

"Claire…"

"I need access to your glutes."

Claire began oiling her hands from bottle number one. It was a progressive process. Each stage required a different mixture. Hot, then cold, then hot. Combined with her magic fingers, when Logan woke up tomorrow, he should feel loose and relaxed, instead of tight and miserable.

"Come on." She patted the padded table. Seeing his continued reluctance, she sighed. "It will be much more serious if I have to maneuver in and out of your shorts. Now, get your ass up here."

"Turn around."

Claire did as Logan asked. *Like a freaking virgin on her honeymoon,* she mumbled under her breath.

"Ready?"

"Yes."

Lying on his stomach, his head faced her way. The small, self-deprecating smile on his face made Claire chuckle. She never could resist a man who was able to laugh at himself.

"What can I say?" he shrugged. "I'm shy."

"I'd tell you I've seen it all before." Claire rubbed her hands together, warming the oil. "I bet I know what you'd say."

"You've never seen mine."

"I'm sure yours is very special."

"That smart mouth must get you in a shitload of trouble."

Claire started on Logan's shoulders. She felt him tense for a second before his muscles began to relax.

"I'm fast and smart," she said. "I either talk my way out or run. So far, it's worked out fine."

"One of these days—"

"Shh." Claire moved to the knots in Logan's back. "Don't talk. Don't think. Let your mind drift and your body relax."

"I can do that."

Claire chuckled. "Then prove it. Mouth. Closed. Mind. Clear."

Her hands were a minor miracle. Logan didn't know when it

happened. Every knot, every ache, every spasm that had racked his body only minutes before, dissolved under her ministrations.

Floating. That was how it felt. The last time he felt so detached from his body was when they pumped him full of drugs after his leg injury. Then he fought the feeling. He couldn't let go of the panic. Deep down, he knew his career hung in the balance.

Today, he had no worries. Claire had his back. Literally. Logan laughed to himself. He felt a strange combination of giddy and calm. Then her thumb worked a particularly tense muscle.

"Holy shit."

The unexpected pain followed by pleasure had his eyes popping open.

"Don't worry," Claire said in a soothing voice. "You aren't a latent masochist. What you're feeling is natural."

"It's freaky how you know what I'm thinking." And reassuring at the same time.

"Your reaction isn't singular, Logan. Men especially get a little anxious that they will start seeking out black leather-clad women who want to be called Mistress Ursula."

"I wouldn't be surprised if some of them already do."

"Undoubtedly." Claire moved to oil number two. "I make it very clear from the start that they won't get that from me."

Now that was a slice of heaven, Logan thought as the sensation of cool replaced heat. Whatever Claire used made his skin sing with gratitude. He was so relaxed he didn't object when she removed the towel covering his backside.

"I'm a professional," Claire said more for her benefit than his.

"For which I am grateful."

Logan's eyes had drifted closed. When Claire didn't resume the massage, he lifted one lid, peeking at her over his shoulder.

"Is there a problem?"

"Forgive me, but I have to say it. That, my friend, is a very fine ass."

Logan hid his smile. He wasn't offended. He was... intrigued. He didn't doubt for a second that this was a first for Claire. She would consider every person she massaged to be a patient. Sexless. As she said, she was a professional. Realizing he could make her step over that line gave his ego a much-needed stroke. The jolt it gave his dick was an unexpected bonus.

Hello, old friend. Logan shifted. The need to accommodate his growing erection made him want to cheer. It seemed the lovely Claire brought *all* of him back to life.

"Logan?"

"Hmm?"

Leaving temptation, Claire walked around the table. Kneeling in front of him, she waited until he shifted his head, until they were eye to eye. His? A deep, relaxed chocolate brown. Hers? A bright, uncertain blue.

"I don't do this." Claire smoothed back his long, dark hair. So thick and soft, she wanted to run her fingers through it. Instead, she lightly massaged his scalp.

"You should." Logan leaned into her touch. "It feels amazing."

Seeing how much he enjoyed what she was doing, Claire added her other hand. Logan sighed. His eyes stayed open. Barely.

"I never comment on a client's ass."

"Have you ever seen one as fine as mine?"

Claire's fingers moved to the base of Logan's neck. The move brought her closer. She could feel his warm, steady breath on her face.

"You aren't going to make this easy, are you?"

"You're the one making it hard, Claire." Logan shifted his hips. No pun intended. "We've already established our attraction. We kissed. Twice."

"I shouldn't bring it here." She looked around the room. "This is my office."

"Office sex happens all the time."

"The Knights won't give me a job if they think I plan on seducing the players."

"I'm not a player," Logan reminded her – and himself. "Not yet."

"I know…"

"One question."

"Okay."

"Are you going to make a habit of this?"

Claire felt her unease drop away. They both knew how ridiculous that sounded. Yes, she hoped this was the start of a long career. As a trainer, not an easy lay for whichever athlete was on her table.

Logan was different. He had been from the moment she read his file. There was something about him. His story spoke to her on a personal level. Small town boy determined to make something of himself. Raw talent didn't get him to the NFL. Work. Sweat. *Heart.*

Having his leg and his dreams smashed had taken the fight out of him. Temporarily. Claire felt deep down inside that she would be the one to help him find it again. It wasn't until she met him that it became more than one professional helping another.

She tugged playfully at his beard. She could plan her life down to the smallest detail. Something like this. The instant attraction. The immediate connection.

This, she could never see coming.

"Claire." He whispered her name.

"Logan." She said his name with absolute conviction.

"I can't make any promises." Leveraging himself onto one elbow, Logan took her hand. "Chances are I'll flame out. No." He stopped her before she could protest. "That isn't negative thinking. I'm through with the self-pity."

"That pity was a good friend for a little while, wasn't it?"

"How do you do that?" Logan kissed her palm. Soft and strong all at once. "How do you know so much about me?"

"I understand how easy it is to embrace those feelings when nothing is going your way. There's something to be said for a constant companion – no matter how destructive."

"It doesn't take long for the *friend* to start eating at your insides. If you and Gaige hadn't shown up, I don't know where I was headed."

"Eventually you would have pulled yourself out of that funk." Claire didn't say it to be kind. She believed in Logan.

"It's nice that one of us is so sure."

"That's the beauty of having a real friend who understands what you're going through." Claire leaned her forehead against his. "You don't have to be strong, or right, or confident all the time. I'm here for you, Logan."

"What about in six months?" Trying to draw in some of her strength, Logan swallowed hard. "What if I fail?"

"I'll still be your friend."

Claire grabbed his beard with both hands. Tugging him close, her mouth covered his. She wasn't in a teasing mood. The kiss was hot. Deep. Instantly sensual. Her tongue tasted, and then retreated when his wanted to play.

"I need more." Logan reached for her.

"Me, too." Rising to her feet, Claire trailed her hand over the long, lean muscles of Logan's back. "Starting back here."

Claire hadn't been exaggerating about Logan's butt. Sexually, her experience wasn't varied. However, in her work, she had seen many, many backsides. As far as she was concerned, it made her somewhat of an expert.

This made it easy for her to say without reservation. Logan Price had a prime ass.

"Brace yourself."

"Why? What? Hey!"

Logan jumped. She bit him! Claire bit his ass! He wasn't sure how he felt about that. Then she lapped at the bite. Her tongue took its time soothing. Caressing. Ratcheting up his desire.

"Sorry." Claire circled the bite with her finger. "It was an impulse I couldn't resist."

"What else can't you resist?"

Claire pulled her shirt over her head.

"Let's find out."

Not wanting to miss anything, Logan rolled onto his back. He enjoyed Claire's eyes on him almost as much as he liked watching her reveal her soft, creamy skin.

"Don't stop now," he urged when she paused at the front clasp of her bra. The swell of her breasts made his mouth water, wondering if they were as sweet as he imagined.

"Woof." Claire's smile widened. "Impressive equipment, Mr. Price."

"I was a bit concerned about that. It's been awhile."

"Impotence?"

Wincing, Logan shook his head. "That isn't a word men like bandied about. I prefer, temporarily uninterested."

As intuitive as she was, there was no way Claire could understand his fear that if the interest returned, he wouldn't be able to perform. Maybe it was Claire. Or it could be he and his body were ready. Perhaps it was a combination of the two. Either way, he felt like he was back – and ready to make the most of it.

Reaching down, Logan gave his cock a long, attention-grabbing stroke. Then one more for good measure.

"You like what you see?"

"Mmm."

"Time to return the favor."

Laughing, Claire slipped the strap off her shoulder. "The old, I've shown you mine, time to show me yours?"

"Every luscious inch."

Play time? Claire liked the idea. She liked trying new things. Before now, her sexual partners had always been by the book. It was… nice. She gave Logan's slowly moving hand another glance. She would bet her first year's salary from the Knights that he knew how to use that thing. Claire almost did a happy dance. Lucky me!

"You're lagging, Claire."

"I can't stop admiring the view."

He might not be professional athlete ripped, but Logan's body was a beautiful thing to behold. Firm muscles. Flat abs. The external obliques that drove women crazy. She included.

Slipping out of her shoes, Claire dropped her shorts before nimbly hopping on the massage table, straddling Logan's hips.

"I knew these would be long and shapely."

Logan's hand ran up her leg from the side of her knee to the edge of her panties. Eyes half closed, he watched with interest as Claire unhooked her bra, letting it slide down her arms and onto the floor. He sucked in his breath with appreciation. A man could live a long time without ever seeing breasts as pretty as hers. His hands cupped the firm mounds. A perfect fit.

With a sigh of pleasure, Claire's head fell forward, her blond hair brushing the top of Logan's hands.

"You like the way I touch you?" He brushed her nipples with the rough pads of his thumbs.

Her sigh became a gasp. Everything felt heavy. Her arms. Her legs. She could barely keep her eyes open. However, closing them was not an option. She wanted to see what Logan was doing with his big, strong hands. What would he do next? She didn't want to miss a second.

Logan sat up, meshing Claire's body with his. Lacing his fingers with hers, he moved her hands behind her back, trapping them, bowing her body until the stiff peaks of her nipples were in easy access for him to savor.

He was in control. After letting his life spiral out of reach for so long, Logan was taking it back – starting now.

"Are you mine?" Logan drew the tip of her breast into his mouth. His teeth scraped the sensitive surface, causing Claire to gasp, her fingers tightening on his.

"For now," Claire breathed.

Now. It was all Logan wanted. Tomorrow was still uncertain. Here.

Now. Claire. The focus of his world had been reduced to this. He sucked harder. *Logan*. His name had never sounded as sweet as when Claire cried out in passion.

"Shit." Breathing deeply, Logan rested his forehead on Claire's chest. "No condoms."

"Shit indeed." Frustrated, Claire tugged until Logan freed her hands. "I knew there was something I forgot when I stocked this room with supplies." She kissed the top of his head. "Silly me for not anticipating sex on the massage table."

Not so silly, Logan thought. He wanted Claire – more than his next breath. However, part of him was glad condoms weren't the first things on her mind. Having sex in the training room wasn't an everyday occurrence. Until now. With him.

"I'm healthy." He should be. It was hard to contract an STD when your only sex partner was your own hand."

"Me too," Claire told him. "But I'm not on the pill. I went off about six months ago."

"There hasn't been any reason to get back on?"

Claire's eyes met his. Steady. Honest. "Not until now. I'll get a new prescription, but it will take a while for it to kick in."

"Note to self. Buy a big box of condoms. Today."

Claire laughed. "More than one." Giving him a long, hard kiss, her hand circled Logan's cock. "I plan to have you soon. And often. Until then. Let me help you with this."

The sight of Claire, naked, straddling his legs was any man's fantasy come to life. Watching her jack him off? It was a wonder he lasted as long as he did. It was only through sheer will, determination, and the hope he wasn't going to suddenly wake up to find this all a cruel dream, that kept him from coming.

Still, Logan was only human. When Claire spread her fingers to accommodate the swipe of her tongue, that was it. With a shout, he felt his release take over. Wave after wave of pleasure coursed through his body.

Logan collapsed onto the table, his arms no longer able to hold his weight. He was spent. Literally and figuratively, there was nothing left in him to give.

"Done in?" Claire asked, leaning over his inert body.

"In the very best sense."

"This is why some people believe the theory that athletes shouldn't have sex the night before competing." She picked up Logan's hand then let it go, laughing when he fell onto the table like a limp noodle.

"Do you buy that?"

"As you know, especially for athletes, it's true if you believe it's true. Personally, I think it's a crock. Those *essential juices* aren't going to make you run faster or throw the ball farther simply because they are still inside of you, instead of me."

Logan lifted one eyelid. God, she was gorgeous. And completely unselfconscious about her nudity. Instead of covering her luscious curves, Claire moved around as if it was the most natural thing in the world.

"Where are you going?" Logan snared her around the waist as she walked by.

"Warm cloth." Claire nodded to the sticky mess on his thighs and stomach.

"It can wait. Let me take care of you." Logan cupped her shapely butt, his other hand sliding between her legs. "Then we can take a shower and clean each other up."

"There isn't time. Your father is expecting us at the bar."

"I'm the boss' son. If we're a few minutes late, he'll cover for me."

"I… Holy crap, Logan."

And he said *her* hands were magic. Logan's fingers slid over her slick folds, unerringly finding all the right places – giving her maximum pleasure. If he hadn't anticipated her reaction, Claire's legs would have given way.

With one hand around her waist and the other doing mind-blowing things between her legs, Logan deftly reversed their positions, lifting Claire onto the table.

"Lean back – but keep your eyes open." Logan brought one wet finger to his mouth. "Mmm. I could make a meal of that. In fact, I think I will."

Easily maneuvering her to the end of the table, Logan lifted her legs, putting one, then the other, on his shoulders. Giving her one last smoldering look, he dove in.

"That—" Claire gasped. God, it felt good. "That should be illegal."

Logan looked up long enough to grin, his tongue slowing, running over his wet lips. "Only if we were in public. Here?" He slid two fingers into her. "I can do anything that makes you happy. Are you happy, Claire?"

Logan didn't wait for an answer. Not that Claire could have given him one. She was too busy gasping with pleasure. Too occupied watching him take her places she hadn't thought possible. Claire ran an encouraging hand through Logan's hair.

"I appreciate a man who enjoys his work," she sighed.

"Not work. Pure pleasure."

"Oh!" Claire felt the beginning of her orgasm. "Yes!" She screamed the word. "I know what you mean."

Every nerve in her body felt like it was exploding into a million pieces. Claire rode the feelings, letting them stretch out over her body. On and on. Never ending.

Please, she thought, *never let it end.*

"That…" Claire slowly came back down to Earth. "You…"

"Shh." Logan kissed the inside of her thigh before gently lowering her legs. "Relax. Don't speak."

He lifted Claire, carrying her across the room to the brand new bathroom. One more thing for which he could thank Gaige.

"How hot do you like your shower water?"

"I can't recall it ever coming up. Hot, but not scalding," Claire said absently. She had too much fun tugging on Logan's beard. "This is so curly." She stretched the hair out several inches.

Logan released Claire's legs so he could reach in the stall.

"Enjoy it while you can. It's coming off."

"Now?"

"There isn't time." Logan guided her into the shower. "If you're still game, you can shave me tomorrow." He put his head under the spray. "How are you at haircuts?"

"One of my specialties." Claire squeezed some shampoo into her palm.

"How did I know you were going to say that?" Logan gave a happy sigh when she started washing his hair. "Is there anything you aren't good at?"

Claire thought about it for a second. Wiping away the trail of soap headed for Logan's eyes, she smiled.

"Taking no for an answer."

"ARE YOU SMILING? You are. Well, hallelujah and saints be praised."

"The bowling league is waiting for their beers, Rhonda."

"Ronnie Balentine and his cronies can wait a few minutes. They won tonight so they're in a good mood. I don't have to guess what's put the bounce in your step." Rhonda looked to the end of the bar where Claire and Jonas were laughing like old friends.

"Ronnie won't leave you a tip if you bring him warm beer."

"Fine." The threat of lost tips always got Rhonda moving. Filling her tray with six glasses, Rhonda took the pitcher of Bud from Logan. "I still want details," she warned before sashaying toward the table of rowdy bowlers.

Logan went back to washing glasses. He had no doubt the little cocktail waitress would find time between serving drinks to grill him about Claire. Not that he minded. Rhonda was an old friend. She had commiserated with his father through the worst of Logan's struggles. Enter a new woman – one who had him humming instead of growling. Anyone, especially someone who cared, would be curious.

Lefty's was jumping. Wednesday was usually slow, but with the bowling tournament just letting out and a group of hunters coming in from a successful trip the tables were almost full. Logan didn't expect it to last. Being a weeknight, the place would probably clear out by ten o'clock.

"Need some help?"

"Let me guess," Logan said as Claire took a seat. "You've tended bar."

Claire nodded. "I make a mean Harvey Wallbanger."

"We don't get much call for those."

"My name isn't Harvey, but I wouldn't say no to banging *you* up against the wall, sweetheart."

Claire rolled her eyes. There was nothing worse than a drunk who thought his charm was only eclipsed by his wit. Glancing at the potbellied jerk three stools to her right, she decided this guy was delusional on both counts. She was about to tell him to keep it to himself when Logan beat her to it.

"Fuck off, Rafer."

A little stronger language than he had planned to use, but Claire appreciated the sentiment.

"Worried the little lady will drop you for a real man, Logan?" Rafer pushed himself and his drink in Claire's direction.

"No."

"What?" Rafer swayed, half off the stool.

"I said no." Claire gave the drunk a withering look. "No to you moving any closer. I can smell you from here, thank you very much. And especially no to banging. Unless I get to bang you over the head with one of these bottles." Not looking at Logan, Claire held out her hand. "Give me your cheapest whiskey. No reason to waste the good stuff on this asshole."

"Come on, Rafer." One of his drinking buddies took him by the arm. "She's not worth the trouble."

"Ya," Rafer let his buddy pull him away. "I can do better. Bitch."

Claire watched the men stagger off. Shaking her head, she grinned at Logan.

"I don't think old Rafer would ever understand that I consider that a compliment."

"I'm sorry about that, Claire."

"Why? You didn't do anything."

Logan kept his eye on Rafer until he had left the bar. The idiot's friends would get him home. Until tomorrow night or the next when Rafer would be back. He was a pain in the ass. One more reason to do his damnedest to get out of Denville. Again.

"Enough about what's his name." Claire shined her brightest smile on Logan. "Are you going to let me back there?"

"Show me what you've got."

For the next few hours, they worked side by side. Of course, Claire knew her stuff. She laughed with Rhonda. Fixed seven mixed drinks all at once without blinking an eye. She even coaxed a laugh out of Wally Nile. The retired schoolteacher was known for his somber personality. Logan didn't know what she said, but whatever it was had the old man chuckling in his beer.

"She's something special."

Jonas handed Logan a tray of empty glasses.

"I know. But…"

"But?"

Logan didn't know how to explain it. It was too soon. He was letting himself believe in the future. One where he played ball again. One where Claire was by his side. After one day? He was setting himself up for a huge fall.

"Claire is here to do a job, Dad." Logan reminded his father, and himself. "One day at a time. Okay?"

"I'm just saying." Jonas slapped Logan on the back. "I knew the moment I saw your mother. Sometimes one look is all it takes."

As if sensing his gaze, Claire looked across the room. Even in the dim lights of the bar, Logan could see the sparkle in her blue eyes. It was like a punch in the heart. Painful and exhilarating.

Just when he thought he was getting his feet back on the ground, a smart, funny, sexy woman came along and knocked him for a loop.

Bad timing? Maybe. Or maybe, Claire Thornton would turn out to be the best thing that ever happened to him.

CHAPTER SEVEN

BY THE TIME Logan and Claire left the bar, it was almost midnight. They had sent Jonas home an hour earlier when it was clear the crowd had cleared out for the evening. The bathrooms and floors were cleaned by the lunch shift so they only had the back bar to wipe down and restock before they locked up and headed home.

Claire rested her head on the bench seat of Logan's old secondhand Ford pickup truck. Everything about the vehicle had seen better days. The paint was scratched. Dents littered both sides. The upholstery was so worn down in spots that the padding poked through. However, it was meticulously clean. Logan polished the truck as though he had gotten it showroom new and planned to keep it that way.

Logan was proud of the old Ford. It was one more thing for Claire to add to the growing list of things she admired about him. His unabashed love for his father. The way he walked Rhonda to her car, making sure she was inside with all four doors locked. That alone earned him major points.

"You worry about Rhonda's ex, don't you?"

Logan shrugged. He turned right onto a street sporadically littered with houses brightly lit with Christmas decorations.

"Most nights, her boyfriend picks her up after work. When he has to work late, I get her to her car. No big deal. Any guy would do the same."

"We both know that isn't true. Your old pal Rafer wouldn't lift a finger to help anyone but himself," Claire said. "From the looks of him, he isn't even doing a very good job of that."

One brief meeting and Claire had Rafer pegged. Logan shouldn't have been surprised. Claire had a way of paring things down to the essentials. People included. Someday, if he could work up the nerve, he might ask her what she saw when she looked at him.

Pulling into his father's driveway, Logan turned off the ignition. For Claire's benefit, he had run the heater on high. Not something he usually did but her look of contentment as the cab warmed to a tropical level made his minor discomfort worth it.

"Want to come up to my place?"

"Still no condoms, remember?"

"There are other things we could do."

Claire winked. "We're really good at those other things. I think you should get some sleep. I have a busy morning planned for you."

"I was talking about sleeping."

As soon as the words left his mouth, Logan knew they were a mistake. What had he said to his father only a few hours earlier? *Too soon.* Instead of taking his own advice, he came across as needy. Whatever it was he and Claire had, they weren't boyfriend and girlfriend. Not yet.

From the look on Claire's face – maybe not ever.

"Logan…"

"Don't." *Please, don't say something kind. Something placating.* That would have killed him. "I jumped ten steps ahead. I'm sorry."

Claire felt a little flutter of panic in her stomach. Sleep with Logan? She hadn't *slept* with anyone since she left home. Sex, yes. She liked that kind of human connection. What Logan mentioned was something else. It was personal. Potentially permanent. Was she ready for that?

For as long as Claire could remember, she wanted… more. More than the little town she grew up in could provide. More than a husband and three kids before she hit twenty-one. Her mother took that path. Then, before she or her sisters were old enough to care, she took off with the first man who could get her away from the choices she made as an eighteen-year-old.

Growing up, Claire's sisters talked about finding a man to take care of them. Someone with a steady job and maybe a few dollars in the bank. Claire kept her mouth shut about her ambitions. The less she said, the less chance anyone could stop her.

The day Claire boarded that bus for the West Coast was the scariest day of her life. It was also the most exhilarating. Succeed or fail, it was all up to her. Her need to make something of herself propelled her. When an obstacle got in her way, she figured out a way around it. When that failed, she had no problem barreling through, the hell with collateral damage.

Men were never a problem. Claire wasn't looking for more than a good time – a way to let off steam. There weren't a great number of ex-lovers but the ones she had never represented anything but a brief fling. She had never met a man who made her want anything more.

Claire felt a chill creeping into the truck. The second Logan saw her shiver, he started the engine, adjusting the heat so it blew full blast her way. The thoughtful gesture brought Claire a sudden, unbidden thought.

If she slowed down for a minute, Logan could be that man. Logan could make her want more. He could make her want it all.

Claire waited for the feeling of panic. And waited. And waited. Turning her head, her eyes met Logan's. All she felt was… happy. Claire smiled. *Well, what do you know?*

"Don't be sorry." Claire wasn't. Her smile grew wider. She wasn't sorry at all. "Can we take it a little slower? I know that's a crazy thing to ask when we've already gotten naked – and more."

"No." Logan took her hand, bringing it to his lips. "We jumped at the attraction. It felt like the right thing to do. Now that it might be something more…" He met her gaze again. "You feel it too?"

Claire nodded.

"Then let's ease off the gas. Neither of is going anywhere."

Inching closer, Claire snuggled into Logan's arms. She rested her head on his shoulder. Had she ever done this? Sat with a man, simply being held without wondering how soon they could have sex so she could leave?

No. This was a first. Wrapping her arms around Logan's waist, Claire sighed.

"This feels good."

"Now who's the mind reader?" Lord, he felt good. She felt the stirring of desire.

"Share the joke?" Logan asked when he heard Claire's chuckle.

"How slow are we talking?"

Logan groaned when he felt Claire's hand slide along his thigh. He shifted his hips as his jeans started to bind in an uncomfortable way.

"Let's say slowish."

"Not glacial."

"God, no." Logan couldn't take that.

"During my bathroom break, I went online and ordered some condoms."

Logan laughed. Leave it to Claire. If he *did* fall in love, this would be a big reason why. She never failed to surprise him.

"Express delivery?"

Claire shook her head. "Seven to ten days."

"That should be about right."

Logan pulled Claire closer – and said a little prayer. *Please, make it seven.*

CHAPTER EIGHT

FIVE DAYS AND counting.

Claire didn't consider the little fib she told Logan as a flat-out lie. Yes, she *had* express-ordered the condoms. However, that was before they had their heart to heart. When they decided to slow things down, telling Logan they had to wait to have sex for at least another week seemed like the right thing to do.

Why put temptation in their path? As it was, they could barely keep their hands off each other. If he knew she had a box of protection hidden away only a few feet from the massage table, Claire doubted it would remain unopened for very long.

Claire was being strong for both of them. And it was driving her crazy.

Sexual frustration was a new experience. From the time she lost her virginity at the ripe old age of twenty, Claire scratched that itch whenever she felt the need.

Sometimes she found a man to help; sometimes she took care of it by herself. *Most* of the time, she took care of it by herself. Logan was the only man she had ever known who made her feel... what was the word?

Antsy. That was it. Thinking about him made her long for his company. Being in the same room with him made her want to touch him. Touching him made her hormones go through the roof.

Her only consolation was that Logan felt the same way. It became more and more difficult to keep things under control. Claire liked holding hands. On the one night Logan hadn't worked late at the bar, she had enjoyed sitting with him in his father's living room watching television with his arm around her.

It was sweet. The kisses they had shared before Logan went to his apartment above the garage were anything but.

Hot. Crazed. Sexual napalm. After Jonas had gone to bed, Claire and Logan attacked each other. Clothing stayed firmly in place. Not that it stopped them from exploring. For their hands, it was a free-for-all. Nothing was off limits.

Claire went with Logan to the bar. They worked side by side. Served drinks. Flirted. Cleaned up. Drove home. Then they would spend an hour or so in the driveway, steaming up the windows of the old Ford.

Between their nightly make-out sessions and the daily massages, Claire could honestly say that she knew Logan's body better than any other man she had ever met. There wasn't an inch she hadn't caressed. She knew where he liked to be touched. Spoiler alert. The answer was… *everywhere.*

Much to her surprise, when it was Logan doing the touching, she felt the same way.

For a couple who planned to slow things down, orgasms were not in short supply. Claire could honestly say that hadn't been the plan. It seemed that once they started, things progressed to their natural conclusion.

Not that they ever lost sight of why Claire had come to Denville. She was proud to say that during their time in the gym, both she and Logan conducted themselves like professionals. Nothing would keep him from making it back as a starter for the Knights. And nothing would keep her from doing everything in her power to get him there.

Logan worked like a man possessed. After the fourth day, his muscles remembered what it was like to follow the routine of a professional athlete. If she hadn't held him back, Logan would have pushed even harder. Claire reminded him that she was the expert. He had to trust her to bring him along at the proper pace. There had to be a progression or he risked hurting himself. An injury at this point could set him back or worse, derail him altogether.

"Slower, Logan." Claire put a hand on the free weight, stopping his upward motion. "This isn't about how many or how fast. It's like sex. The more time you take going up and down, the better."

"Christ, Claire." Logan shot her a disbelieving look. "I almost dropped this sucker on my foot. Save the sex talk for when I don't have thirty pounds of solid iron in each hand."

"Sorry. Forget I'm here. One more set of ten."

Claire circled Logan, observing his technique. She wanted to make sure the weight was neither too heavy nor too light. Noting his movement was smooth and easy, she stood back and admired the view.

For her, there wasn't anything sexier than a fit man pushing his body to the limits. Unless that man was Logan.

He still sported the long hair and beard. Though Claire looked forward to seeing his clean-shaven face, she had to admit there was a certain appeal to his current look. Rugged. Manly.

Sweat saturated Logan's gray t-shirt. A corresponding dark line ran down the back of his baggy shorts. Now, all Claire wanted to do was lick the salty heat of his skin – every firm, muscular inch of it. Her mouth watered as she watched his arms flex, straining as he finished the final rep.

Claire breathed as hard as Logan, but for a very different reason. Today was the day. Time to speed things up. Those condoms were finally going to see the light of day.

"Are we done?"

Unaware that he was about to get lucky, Logan lowered the barbells to the ground.

"Good work, Logan. Put the weights away, and then hop up on the table."

Surreptitiously, Claire slipped a few foil packets out of their box, putting them into the pocket of her sweats. She filled a tray with the usual creams and oils before closing the cupboard.

"Aren't you going to tell me to get naked?"

"At this point, that should go without saying."

Having already toed off his shoes, Logan toyed with the band of his shorts, a crooked grin on his lips.

"I like hearing it."

So he wanted to play. Claire was fine with that. Setting the tray by the table, she put her hands on her hips, giving him a long, thorough once over. *My, oh, my. He was fine indeed.*

"Off with the shirt and drop the shorts, Price. Let me see what you've got."

"I'm packing, Ms. Thornton."

Claire's gaze dropped to the noticeable bulge between his legs. She licked her lips in anticipation.

"That must be painful. It might be better if we start with you face up today. I wouldn't want you to hurt yourself."

Logan shed his clothes without further delay. He was on his back before Claire could do more than smile at his alacrity. Just as eager, she picked the bottle of lotion she had been saving for just this occasion.

"You should be proud of your progress, Logan." Claire warmed the cream in her hand. "In less than a week I've seen real progress in the flexibility and strength in your knee."

Moving to the head of the table, Claire massaged Logan's temples.

"Your program is the reason." Logan sighed with pleasure. "Nothing I tried on my own had anything close to this kind of success. You should be proud of yourself, Claire. This program has the potential to help a lot of people. Not just athletes."

Claire's hands moved down Logan's neck, smoothing the knotted cords. Reaching as many people as possible was her ultimate goal. She had dreams of clinics all over the world where trained associates would bring a better quality of life to their patients. Gaige had let her start the dream. Her time with Logan expanded it on a daily basis.

The progress they made with his body was a big part of it. Then there was the personal side. Logan listened. He wasn't all about himself, his problems, or his injury. He encouraged her to share her own deepest hopes and fears.

In the short time she had known Logan Price, Claire had opened up in a way she never thought possible. She told him about her childhood in Iowa. The abandonment of her mother, her distant father. The fact that she hadn't kept in touch with her family.

For the first time, Claire realized how much of that pain she still carried with her. And how talking about it, with Logan, lightened a place deep inside. A place she had avoided for way too long.

"That smell." Logan took a deep breath. "Mmm. It's new." He breathed in again. "Nice. What is it?"

Pleased that he noticed, Claire smiled.

"It's my own blend. Citrus, mainly. A blend of herbs and spices. And," Claire whispered in his ear, "a secret ingredient."

"Something else is different."

Logan rolled his head in a slow circle. As always, Claire's ointments, combined with her magic hands, soothed his muscles. Relaxed his mind. Stirred his body. However, today he felt... more. The fragrance filled his senses.

No, not filled. Cleared. That was it. While his body relaxed, his mind became sharper. He was attuned to her every touch. Before, as Claire massaged his tired muscles, his mind would float. Today, it focused on what she was doing. It was almost as though *he* was probing his flesh – assisting. Crazy. That wasn't possible. Was it?

"It isn't a hallucinogen, if that's what you're worried about."

"Not worried. Curious."

Logan slowly opened his eyes, his gaze meeting Claire's. The instant, startling connection made them both gasp.

What the hell?

"Claire—"

"I don't know, Logan." Claire began massaging his arm, moving to the side of the table, her eyes remaining locked with his. "This is a new blend. The idea is to focus the patient's mind. I have a theory that if a person can picture a specific place that needs healing, their mind can aid in the process. The herbs and spices are meant to be a natural aid to help the brain concentrate."

Claire smoothed the cream over Logan's hand. She laced her fingers with his.

"This isn't just concentration," Logan said. He tugged until she sat on the table. Hands still joined, he kissed the back of hers before resting them on his chest.

Over his heart, Claire noticed. She was certain it was an unconscious gesture.

"Has anyone else used the lotion?"

Claire nodded. "I tested it on a few friends. I gave them all a sample and a questionnaire. It was very informal."

"And?" Logan rubbed a circular pattern on the back of her hand with his thumb. "What were the results?"

"Encouraging," Claire said. "They all reported greater concentration. I hoped to do something official at UW next fall. If the grant I've applied for comes through. It will be tight, if I get the Knights job, but I can do both."

Logan didn't doubt it for a second. Claire had drive and ambition – with the talent to back them up. What he wanted to know right now was what the hell was happening between them?

"This didn't happen to anyone else?"

"Not even close. We seem to be unique."

"I could have told you that." Logan slipped his fingers into her hair, pulling her face close to his. "I'm not going to use the cream as an excuse, Claire. Our connection has been there from day one." He softly kissed her. "Maybe your concoction heightened it. It didn't create it."

Claire felt Logan's challenge. He dared her to excuse it away. Claire did not intend to do so. She knew when something was real or an illusion. This was the realest she had ever felt. Not because of the cream, because of Logan.

This time, when they kissed, it was deeper, stronger than ever before. Claire let go, falling into the moment. The outside world ceased to exist.

"You've been very patient," she whispered, her lips leaving his to trail along his firm jaw. She glanced at his erection. Impressive. "I need, Logan. Now."

Claire transferred the condom from her pocket to Logan's hand. She wasn't going to get all cute at this stage. He was much more experienced at putting one on than she was. They could play with that some other time. Today, she didn't want any mishaps that would slow them down.

"It's been a while," Logan said with a teasing smile. Belying his words, in no time flat, he had the packet open. Deftly, he rolled on the condom. "Guess it's like riding a bike."

"I'm not going there. I never found a bicycle seat very comfortable."

Claire undressed quickly. In her haste, her sports bra went sailing across the room, landing neatly on the doorknob.

"Bet you couldn't do that again if you had a hundred shots."

"Do you want to watch me toss my bra while we play a weird game of horseshoes, or do you want this?" Claire took hold of his erection. "Inside of me."

Logan's answer took her breath away. In a flash, their positions were reversed. Flat on her back, Claire let out a delighted laugh.

"Move that fast on the football field and you'll be an all-star in no time."

Logan nuzzled Claire's neck. He knew what she liked. There was a spot, just behind her right ear that if he bit, she would...

"Logan!"

...go crazy. He smiled against her soft, fragrant skin. The sound of Claire's passion was the most potent aphrodisiac. Better than any drug. Natural. Strong. Addictive. Now that he'd had a taste, he never wanted to give it up.

"Speaking of having a taste."

"Mmm," Claire sighed. "Were we speaking of that?"

"Where's your mind reading ability?"

"It stops working when you do things like that. My whole brain short circuits."

"That's fine. You don't have to think about this. Just feel."

That she could do. Happily.

Claire raised her arms over her head, gripping the table. Her fingers dug into the soft leather. The position left the long length of her body open to Logan and his wicked, wonderful mouth.

"Why do you taste better than anyone I've ever known?"

Logan asked the question while making a feast of her breasts. He ran his tongue between gently sloping mounds before drawing one hard, cherry-colored nipple into his mouth.

"It's the herbs." She gasped the words. He wanted to ask questions? Now? How was she supposed to answer when her brain swirled a haze of pleasure?

"The same ones you give me every morning?" Logan bit her sensitive flesh, sending a jolt through her entire body then centering between her legs. "I like the smoothie. Vanilla and…?"

"Mint!" Claire cried out when his fingers pinched the other nipple.

"Right," Logan whispered against her skin, "Spread your legs, Claire."

That sounded good. Claire welcomed Logan's weight. She ran her foot up the length of his calf. The coarse hair against the sensitive bottom of her foot was one more stimulant, one more building block to the growing pressure inside of her.

"You are so slick." Logan teased her, the tip of his erection sliding up and down her folds. He ran a finger between her legs, holding her gaze as he slowly licked off the juices. "It can't just be the herbs. It's you, Claire. Sweet, sweet Claire."

His mouth took hers. She could taste a bit of herself, but Logan's flavor burst across her tongue. Claire would know it anywhere. Blindfolded, if she were asked to kiss a hundred men, she would pick him in an instant.

"Open your eyes, Claire."

"Hmm?" Claire did as Logan asked as her tongue gathered one more taste from her lips.

"Watch. Stay with me."

Logan slowly entered her body. Inch by tantalizing, agonizing inch.

Claire tried to urge him on, her legs twining with his, her hips pushing forward. She was strong, but Logan was stronger. He controlled the pace. The dark, rich color of his eyes looked almost molten, holding her gaze.

Mine.

For a moment, Claire thought he said it aloud, so clear was the word. Logan rotated his hips, the angle of his entry shifting slightly until he was deep, deep inside of her.

"Can you feel that, Claire?" Logan demanded, his breath rushing over her face. "Tell me it feels good. Tell me you never want it to end."

"Never, Logan. Never."

With a grunt of satisfaction, Logan's thrust became harder, faster. The release they both craved came rushing at them in a downpour that burst over them at the same moment. Bright lights danced in front of Claire's eyes. They seemed to come directly from Logan. Another gift from this extraordinary man.

As he had on the way up, Logan held her as she floated back down to Earth. His strong arms wrapping around her. He gently disengaged from her body, yet Claire still felt connected. There were no words to explain it. She just knew. With Logan, she would never be alone again.

CHAPTER NINE

THE STEAM FROM their recent shower filled the bathroom air. Claire walked around Logan, lifting his hair. Wet, it hung several inches past his shoulders. Thick and healthy, she had become fond of running her fingers through it whenever the impulse hit her.

With a sigh, Claire picked up Logan's comb.

"Are you sure about this?"

"It's my hair. My beard. My decision."

"I know."

"Then what's the problem?"

Claire didn't know. She had known for some time that this moment would come. She thought the beard would go before Christmas. Then when New Year's passed and the subject hadn't come up again, she figured he'd changed his mind.

A cold, wet January was followed by a windy February, and then a strangely mild March. It was the middle of April. Claire and Logan's routine was a satisfactory one. They worked out every day. Shared meals, went for runs. They spent almost every evening at *Lefty's Pub* – every night in each other's arms.

No one questioned Claire's presence. She eased into Denville like a native. Jonas accepted her. That was clear. The change in Logan since her arrival had been remarked upon by more than one person.

In truth, the whole town was amazed at the transformation. Gone was the grumpy, forlorn ex-football star. In his place, a man who seemed to be embracing his life. The dark circles were gone from under his eyes. His body had filled out, losing that lean, gaunt look. Best of all,

Logan no longer ran in the middle of the night. Those days were a thing of the past.

The residents of Denville attributed all of this to Claire.

What surprised Claire was how much she enjoyed small town life. She liked getting her gossip from Rhonda. The waitress was never at a loss for new information – always delivered with a lack of cattiness that she admired. Rhonda liked to talk. Talking about her neighbors was second nature. There was nothing malicious about it. She was simply spreading the news

When Gaige talked Claire into spending six months in the sticks, making a new friend hadn't seemed likely. Rhonda was a bonus. Along with Logan, this assignment had turned into more than she ever dreamed.

She liked Denville. She liked Rhonda. And surprise, surprise, she liked Logan's beard.

"If you really want to get rid of it, I'm happy to oblige. It's just…"

Logan sat on a chair, a large bath towel around his neck. Claire had used a safety pin to hold it in place.

"What?"

"Why now?"

"It feels right." Logan shrugged. "I can see the end, Claire. In December, training camp seemed so far away. No matter what I told myself, I wasn't ready to believe. Not entirely."

"We've known each other four months."

"The best four months of my life." Logan took her hand. "You brought me back to life, Claire. When I woke up this morning, I knew it was time to take the next step."

Suddenly, Claire understood. The beard represented the Logan who had given up. Now that he truly believed, there was no longer a place for it in his life.

Claire picked up the trashcan, handing it to him.

"Hold this under your chin." With the scissors, she made the first cut. "Time to stop hiding."

It had been a while since she shaved a man. Almost ten years by her estimation. Luckily for Logan's face, the process came back to her quickly. Once the longer hair was trimmed, she lathered his face.

The brand new safety razor removed the hair with little problem. By the time she was halfway through, Claire had found her rhythm. She ran her hand over the shaved skin. Smooth as silk. And not a nick in sight.

"I'm surprised you're so calm." Claire moved to the other side of Logan's face.

"Why?"

"I have a sharp object in my hand. If I slipped, the loss of blood could be significant."

Logan tipped his head to the side. Eyes closed, he was completely relaxed. For months, he had trusted Claire with his future. The results were beyond his wildest imagination. She shared his bed. His home. His life. Letting her near his throat with a razor seemed as natural as breathing.

"You have a steady hand, Claire." Logan lifted one eyelid. "You don't look nervous."

"I'm not."

Claire surprised him by closing her mouth over his. Automatically, Logan's hands went to her hips.

"Time to play?" he asked. As always, his body's response to her was instantaneous.

"No." Claire pulled back. "Just a thank you for trusting me."

"Well, thank *you*."

Claire resumed shaving him, humming some happy tune.

"I do, you know."

She paused the razor under his nose.

"You do? Do what?"

"Trust you."

Claire smiled. "I know."

"You can trust me."

Frowning, she stepped back. "You don't think I do?"

Logan hadn't planned to start this conversation now. He'd been thinking about it for several weeks. Claire was such an open person. She was funny and bright. She made friends easily. His father adored her. And Logan...? He couldn't imagine his life without her.

For all that, Logan didn't know how Claire felt. Not really. He wanted to delve into her feelings. However, that would mean putting his on the table. He put his body in her hands every day. He didn't know if he was ready to put his heart out there. The thought that she might not feel the same was terrifying. Scarier than a three-hundred-pound linebacker. Until he felt on steadier ground with his emotions, he wasn't going to take any chances.

"I know you trust me, Claire." Logan patted her on the butt. "My career is tied with yours. If I fail, you fail."

"True." Claire looked at Logan again. Something else was going on. Some hidden meaning beneath his words. For the life of her, she didn't know what it was.

"Almost finished?" Logan wanted to move the conversation along. That speculative look in Claire's eyes made him nervous.

"That's it. Let me wipe off the last of the shaving lotion. There." Claire stood back to get a good look.

Logan waited for Claire's reaction. He had never considered himself a particularly vain man. Women had always found him attractive. The last time he really looked at himself in the mirror was just after his injury.

True, his frame of mind hadn't been the best, and all kinds of drugs were still in his system. All that said, he remembered seeing a man that wouldn't scare off animals or frighten young children.

"Well?" Logan asked. "Say something. Is there some kind of hideous growth that I wasn't aware of?" Logan ran his hand over his face. There were times when the thing itched like crazy.

"What time do we have to be at the bar?"

Logan frowned. What the hell did the bar have to do with his face?

"In about an hour. Why?"

Claire grabbed his hand, pulling him out of his chair and into the workout room.

"That should give us enough time."

She disposed of the towel around his neck, and then jumped into his arms, her legs wrapping around his waist. Claire kissed him. Hard and long. When she finally pulled away, they were both breathing hard.

"I guess you like the way I look."

"You'll do."

Claire rained kisses over his freshly shaved face. It wasn't just a good-looking face. It was gorgeous. She had grown fond of the beard. It made him look outdoorsy. Rugged. There was nothing wrong with that – there was a definite appeal.

One look at him without it? Claire was ready to buy him a lifetime supply of razors – she didn't want to take any chances that he would cover up his face again.

"You have dimples." Claire licked each indention.

"I take it you're a fan?"

"I never thought about it before. I am now."

Claire tugged at his damp hair, angling Logan's head. Now that was a jaw line. Her lips traced the firm line. Smooth. Sexy as hell.

"It was a crime to cover this face."

"You liked it well enough before."

"I did. This is new. Different." With a happy hum, Claire kissed him again.

Logan loved all the attention. He'd had women tell him he was good looking. Claire's reaction made him feel like a movie star. From now on, he planned to shave every morning without fail.

"On the floor. Now. And lose the jeans."

Doing as she commanded, Logan waited on his back while Claire undressed. Happily, they had passed the condom stage. Since they were exclusive and Claire was on the pill, there was no longer a need for any barriers during sex.

It was a first for Logan. He had been sexually active since the age of sixteen. Back then, it was all about making sure the girl didn't get pregnant. With his ambitions, the last thing he needed was to be tied down. Later, staying away from STDs was added to his fastidious precautions.

Sex without a condom was amazing. Or maybe it was sex with Claire. Either way, it was a heady, addictive combination.

"What about my haircut?" Logan asked with a grin as Claire straddled his hips. He was ready and so was she. In one fluid movement, she slid down his length, her eyes locked with his.

"We'll have time for that." She started to move. "This won't take long."

WOLF WHISTLES GREETED Logan when he walked into *Lefty's Pub* an hour later.

"What the hell, Price?" Barney Todd called out from his usual spot at the end of the bar. "When did you take the pretty pills?"

Logan took the comment in stride. Barney played center back in high school. He was now one of the most successful realtors in the panhandle. His work took him on the road a lot, but whenever he was in town, he made the bar his main hangout. Unlike Rafer, he was a friend, then and now. A little ribbing was natural, and it went both ways.

"Jealousy is an ugly thing, Barney. Oh, sorry. That isn't jealousy, it's your face."

The other patrons whooped over Logan's joke. Barney flipped Logan the bird, along with a smile. Logan sent a free drink Barney's way.

"I can't believe my eyes."

Rhonda set her tray on the bar so she could run her hands over Logan's face. Because he was fond of her, he didn't protest. His eyes met Claire's warm gaze. The memory of their fast and furious lovemaking brought a huge smile to his face.

Claire had been right. It didn't take long. But, oh, baby, it felt good. A naked woman taking her pleasure, giving it back. If there was a better way to spend five minutes, Logan didn't know what it was.

"I know that look," Rhonda said, her fingers mussing what was left of Logan's hair. "And it isn't for me."

"Damn straight, it isn't. Pug would have my hide if I ever looked at you that way."

"Pug isn't a man easily riled." Chuckling, Rhonda retrieved the tray. "Fooling with his woman will do it, though."

"Hey," Logan called out. "That reminds me. Did Elmer sign the papers?"

The whole custody bugaboo had been hanging on for months. Elmer was determined to cause as much trouble as possible for his ex-wife. He didn't want their children. However, the idea of Rhonda having a happy life with another man drove him crazy.

Every attempt to get Elmer to drop the lawsuit had failed. Pug talked to him. Which only made Elmer more determined, especially when Pug showed up in his uniform. The other residents of the trailer park gave Elmer grief for days over that.

Logan attempted to reason with the man. Another dead end. Elmer saw Logan as the Denville elite – as if there was such a thing. No one in Denville had money. There were no grand houses. Weekly bowling and PTA meetings were what passed for society.

The only thing that set Logan apart was football. Since he was never any good at it, in Elmer's eyes, it was enough.

Elmer's mother finally got things moving in the right direction. Never a fan of Rhonda, the lawsuit was something the old woman encouraged – at first. Then it was pointed out that if Elmer somehow won, *she* would be the one looking after his children.

That was enough for Abilene Sykes. She liked her cigarettes, her gin rummy, and her Jack Daniels. She did not like children. Not even her own.

A few sharp words in Elmer's ear and the suit was dropped. Rhonda had her lawyer draw papers not only getting Elmer to relinquish all claim to the children, but they also made it possible for Pug to adopt them. By Christmas, they would be one big happy family.

"Look." Rhonda waved her finger in front of Logan's face.

"Is that what I think it is?" Taking her hand, Logan dutifully admired the modest diamond ring.

"It's beautiful, Rhonda." Logan kissed her cheek. "No one deserves a happily ever after more than you and Pug."

Rhonda held out her hand, admiring the little glint of light that reflected off her engagement ring. It wasn't a big rock by any definition. For Rhonda, it was better than the one Elmer gave her. It certainly meant more. She was going to marry big, sweet, steady Stanley Doughtry. And she was holding on, no matter what. This time, she had found the true love of her life.

"Hey," Logan lifted Rhonda's chin. "What's with the tears?"

"I…" Rhonda choked out the word.

"Men." Claire joined them, slipping a comforting arm around Rhonda's shoulder. "Why can't they ever recognize happy tears? Come on, Rhonda. Let's get away from all this testosterone so you can tell me every detail of how Pug proposed."

"I proposed," Rhonda laughed through her tears. "Pug bought the ring months ago, but was too shy to ask."

"Even better," Claire said, leading Rhonda to an empty booth.

"What did I do?" Logan threw up his arms. He looked to the other men at the bar for commiseration. "Didn't I congratulate her?"

"Don't try to figure them out, Logan." Cyrus Welliver called out. Of all the men in the place, Cyrus had the most experience with marriage. He was on wife number five. "I can't tell one tear from another. Angry. Happy. Sad. Greeting Card commercial. Who the hell knows?"

While the rest of the crowd chimed in, including Cyrus' wife, Logan checked the bar, making sure it was fully stocked for the evening. All the while, he kept one eye on Claire and Rhonda.

Bent together over the ring, Claire's blond head, Rhonda's dark one, they laughed at something. As always, the sound made Logan smile. Claire laughed a lot. She was a naturally happy person, just one of the things that drew him to her.

Even on his best days, Logan tended to keep his emotions inside. He could celebrate with the best of them. The day Denville High won the state championship. When he won that full-ride scholarship his sophomore year at Ohio State. Having his name called out during the NFL draft. Those were occasions. He was bound to be exuberant then.

Logan thought about day-to-day life. There weren't that many moments in a regular day that warranted smiles and laughter. He got up, he went about his business, and he went to bed. Was he happy? Sure. Did he smile at the sound of rain on the roof or laugh at the sight of a robin building its nest? Probably not. Claire did. And Logan smiled and laughed with her.

How could he not want to have all that light and joy near him? Now that he'd had it, how could he contemplate life without it? Claire had become essential.

Logan wondered. What did Claire think when she looked at Rhonda's engagement ring? Was she simply happy for a friend? Or did part of her long for the same thing? Was she thinking ahead? Did she see a future with him or did she see herself moving on when they were back in Seattle?

Too many questions for which Logan had no answers. Two months. The plan was for them to spend a few weeks in Seattle before training camp started in July. What had once seemed so far away now came at him like a bullet train.

His body was in the best shape of his life. Fit, inside and out thanks to Claire's hard work. She made sure he exercised properly. Ate right. Got plenty of sleep. Then there was the sex. Nothing loosened you up like a love life filled with passion and spontaneity.

Today was a perfect example. Claire made every day an adventure. When she wanted him, she let him know. When he wanted her, she was more than happy to jump in with both feet. Intense, playful. The sex ran the gamut. Knowing he could have her whenever he wanted added one big fat cherry to his monster sundae.

Logan was ready to make his comeback. He wasn't ready to lose Claire.

Since there was no stopping time, all he could do was ride this out. He had no idea what the conclusion would be. Would he make the team? Would Claire walk away?

Stop thinking! Enjoy each moment. That's what Claire would tell him if she knew the jumble going on in his brain.

Enjoy me while you've got me.

"Hey, Logan. How about another draft?"

"Coming right up."

Logan grabbed a glass from the cooler. That's what Logan would do. Enjoy Claire. He would take what she so generously gave him. And he would do his best to make her want to stay.

CHAPTER TEN

"THANKS FOR MEETING me."

"I'm honored that you asked. Picking out a wedding dress is a huge deal."

"Even if it's online shopping."

Rhonda opened her laptop on the kitchen counter. She shared the house Pug inherited from his uncle about five years ago. Being busy, and a good old Oklahoma boy, little had been done to update the interior. It sported the same avocado green everything from back when avocado green was all the rage.

Now that Rhonda was the woman of the house, things were going to change. Slowly. A little paint here. A throw rug there. She wasn't in a hurry. She and Pug had the rest of their lives to get it right. Just in time for the next generation to come along and change it to their tastes.

That was how it should be. The circle of life. Why that circle ever included avocado green, Rhonda would never understand.

"I had the big, white wedding the first time." Rhonda snorted. "Not that I walked down the aisle a virgin. That horse had left the barn long before. Here."

Rhonda pulled up a picture on the screen of her wedding day. All the pictures of Elmer were long gone. But she kept a few to show her children, then someday her grandchildren.

"Wow," Claire said, struggling for a diplomatic comment. "That's…"

"Go ahead and say it. I look like I was eaten by a cotton ball."

"A cotton ball with ruffles. Lots and lots of ruffles."

Rhonda laughed. "It was my dream gown. Looking at it now, I realize it was more of a nightmare. The *dress* and the marriage."

Claire gave Rhonda's hand a sympathetic squeeze.

"You got out. That's what's important. You have two beautiful children and a man who adores you. I'd say, in the long run, you came out the winner."

"I did," Rhonda beamed. "This time, I'm going classic. Simple. Uncomplicated. Just like my man."

"Sounds perfect."

Claire sipped her coffee, watching as dress after dress scrolled by. Some were hard to look at without wincing. Apparently, ruffled cotton balls never went out of style.

"Let's try a different website." Rhonda tapped away at the keys. "How about you and Logan. Any wedding plans."

Claire spat out her mouthful of coffee, barely missing the computer. "Why in the world would you ask that?"

Rhonda handed her a napkin.

"You've been here for quite a while."

"Four months," Claire said. "That isn't very long."

"You knew each other from before, right?"

"Right."

Claire hated to lie. The story was one they settled on before she got to know Rhonda. Keeping the secret was Logan's decision – one Claire respected. The day might come when she could come clean to her new friend. This wasn't that day.

"A blind man could see how things are between the two of you."

"How are they?" Claire was curious what Rhonda saw.

"You fit. He's back to the Logan we all knew in high school."

"That isn't all on me, Rhonda. Logan wanted to pull out of his funk."

"But he didn't know how until you came to Denville." Rhonda's earnest expression made Claire a little uncomfortable. Claire knew she liked Logan. No, that wasn't fair. This had passed the like stage long ago. They had fun. They had sex like she never dreamed existed. Anything more? Claire wasn't sure she knew what *more* was.

Claire didn't believe in blaming her parents for her hang-ups. So her mother left when she was in diapers. Her father forgot he had daughters most of the time.

Sometimes she had to wonder why some people had kids. Her

mother and father were prime examples. That said – they were who they were. By the time she had reached adulthood, it was time to find out who she was, not who her parents made her.

So why did she have a lump in her stomach when she thought about a future with Logan? She would like to think it was because she wasn't ready. After so many years focused on one goal, now that it was a whisper's breath away, did she want to get serious about anyone? Even Logan?

The nasty little voice in her head that only came out when she felt vulnerable, told a different tale. A woman who was raised by loving, nurturing parents would jump if she felt half of what Claire did for Logan.

Being honest with herself wasn't always easy. In this case, Claire knew it was vital. She *was* a product of her upbringing. Her parents *had* screwed with her head. Right now, she and Logan neared the end of a huge journey. If there was more to them – together – the time to decide wasn't now.

Claire felt the knot in her stomach loosen. She wasn't much of a *put off until tomorrow* kind of woman. However, in this case, it was all she could do. Logan didn't need her drama added on to his own.

After he makes the team. That would be soon enough to evaluate her feelings. And his.

"I'm too nosy," Rhonda sighed. "It's my biggest failing."

"I like it when you push for information," Claire said. Then she winked. "When you're pushing someone else."

Rhonda laughed, relieved that she hadn't offended Claire.

"You and Logan are the only tough nuts in Denville. Anyone else, all I have to do is ask *how ya doin', hun*? I get a rundown of every minute detail."

"Which you then share with me. I'm good with that." Claire clicked on a dress, gasping when she saw it magnified. Excited, she turned the screen toward Rhonda. "Ta da."

With a gasp, Rhonda clapped a hand over her mouth. Her eyes met Claire's, filling with tears.

"That's it. How did you know that was it?"

"One look and it screamed *Rhonda*."

The pale pink floor-length gown was as far away from poofy ruffles as she could get. A simple lace sheath. Elegant. Perfect for Rhonda's subtle curves and dark hair.

"Pug's chin will hit the ground when he sees me in this." Rhonda was already pulling out her credit card. "We need something similar for you. Knee-length. Blue. To compliment your eyes."

"Me?"

"Oh, crap. I got so far ahead of myself I forgot to ask. You'll be my maid of honor, won't you? Pug already asked his brother to be best man."

"I don't know, Rhonda. Isn't there someone you're closer to? Or maybe a family member?"

"Mama's my only family." Rhonda rolled her eyes. "She'll come to the wedding because it will look bad if she doesn't. Though just yesterday she was trying to talk me into going back to Elmer."

"No." What the hell was wrong with Rhonda's mama? Who wanted their daughter to be treated like a punching bag?

"Yes," Rhonda sighed. "'Marriage is for life, Rhonda. In the eyes of God, Elmer will always be your husband.'"

"Yikes," Claire cringed. "God, marriage, and life. Three biggies. Was that supposed to be a guilt trip?"

"Probably. It worked once." Rhonda ran her tongue over the implant that had replaced her knocked-out tooth. "Since then, she's like a broken record."

"I admire you, Rhonda. Leaving an abusive relationship takes a lot of inner strength."

"It's what millions of women do every day."

"And millions don't." Claire frowned. "Christ, how screwed up is that? Millions."

"I know. I'm sorry I brought it up." Rhonda slapped her hand on the counter. "Enough sad talk. This is a happy occasion. And you didn't answer my question."

Since she couldn't tell Rhonda the real reason she had come to Denville, she couldn't explain that she would soon be leaving. The web of lies lured in more and more people.

"Have you set a date?"

"Why? Are you planning to leave town?" Rhonda tone teased until she saw the look on Claire's face. "Oh, my God. *Are* you leaving? Does Logan know? When? Why? Will it be for good? How could you?"

Any guilt Claire felt quickly dissipated in the face of Rhonda's over the top response. For a moment, she found herself laughing too hard to respond.

"This isn't funny, Claire." Rhonda's lips twitched. "Damn it, stop laughing."

"I will as soon as you do."

"*I'm* not."

Rhonda tried, but she couldn't hold out. Soon, she and Claire were laughing so hard, tears ran down their faces. This went on for several minutes. Finally, they calmed down enough to wipe at their wet cheeks.

"Fine." Breathless, Rhonda handed Claire a tissue. "I may have overreacted a bit."

"Just a little." Claire was still smiling when she explained. "I get it, Rhonda. You're worried that I'm going to abandon Logan. He'll fall into a deep depression – one he'll never crawl out of. The beard will return. He'll start collecting stray cats."

"Enough," Rhonda chuckled. "You can't blame me, Claire. Logan is an important person in my life. I worry about him. *Are* you leaving?"

Claire needed to discuss this with Logan. Rhonda was a gossip. However, when it came to something important, she could keep it locked up tighter than Fort Knox. If he was ready, it might be time to share what was going on. At least with a select few.

"If the day comes that I need to leave Denville, Logan will be the first to know. I won't sneak away. That's all I can say for now, Rhonda."

"Is there a problem?" Rhonda took Claire's hand. "You don't have to share the details. I want you to know I'm here if you need me."

Claire felt close to tears again, but they had nothing to do with silly laughter. Rhonda wasn't just her friend. She was her... *friend*. A confidant. Try as she might, Claire couldn't remember if she ever had one of those before she came to Denville. Now, in the span of a few months, she had two.

Rhonda was like a sister. Better. Claire's sisters by blood were scattered to the wind. Before that, none of them had been close. She now knew what it was like to be close to another woman. Someone to share silly jokes with. To shop with.

If Rhonda was her friend, Logan was her... *best friend*. Claire knew without hesitation, Logan was the first person she would go to if she were in trouble. Or had something good to share. Or simply wanted to hang out.

He was the man she— That was where Claire cut herself off. The word love flitted briefly through her brain. *Too soon*, she screamed silently. *If ever.*

"Are you okay?" Rhonda asked, frowning. "You're looking a little green around the gills." Rhonda gasped. "Are you pregnant? I felt the same way the first time. I couldn't hold anything down and—"

"Stop. God, Rhonda. First, you have me skulking out of town, and now, I'm pregnant. Once and for all. It's no to both. Absolutely. No doubt about it. There will be no unplanned little Logans running around in nine months."

"Or eight."

"Rhonda!"

"Would it be so terrible?" Rhonda sighed. "Babies are lovely. Pug and I plan on at least two. Maybe more."

"I don't want children."

"What?" Rhonda screeched. "Never?"

Rhonda's cry of outrage shot straight through Claire's eyeball. It was painful, yet somehow comical. This time, she kept her laughter to herself. It seemed Rhonda fell into that group of people who thought every woman longed to be a mother. Claire hated to break it to her friend, but that simply wasn't true. At least not for Claire. Not now.

"I don't see myself as terribly maternal, Rhonda. Would it be fair to have a baby hoping I would feel different after it was here?"

"No," Rhonda conceded. "You could change your mind. You're young."

"I'm not ruling out the possibility. When my life is more fixed, there's a chance I'll want to get pregnant." When Rhonda started to speak, Claire quickly added, "That day is a long way off."

"Why? I don't mean the baby part. Why isn't your life fixed? What are you waiting for, Claire?" When Claire didn't answer, Rhonda shook her head. "Okay. You don't have to tell me. Just remember. Putting your life on hold, while you wait for something to happen, means you're losing precious time you can never get back. I could have married Pug a year ago but told him it was too soon."

"Maybe it was."

"Too soon for what?" Rhonda demanded. "To be with the man I love? To be a real family? Nothing has changed in twelve months, Claire. I knew it wouldn't. I let my lingering doubts, and stupid worries about what other people would think, stop me."

"I've never worried about what other people think." Claire could say that one thing without reservation.

"I'm getting there," Rhonda said with a touch of envy. "I've narrowed it down to about a quarter of Denville and Pug. When I am able to say the only opinion, other than my own, that I care about is my future husband's, I'll be golden."

"You grew up here," Claire reasoned. "When you know people that long, you can't help but be influenced by what they think."

"Is that why you left Iowa? To get away from small town ideas?"

Yes. Except Claire had never cared what her hometown thought of her. Blinders and earplugs. She put them on the day she decided to get out. If she had stopped to look around, she might have found a friend like Rhonda.

Was that part of the reason she blocked everyone out? If there had been even one person to care about when she was growing up, would it have made leaving harder?

The day Claire left Iowa, she did so without a single regret. She knew that wouldn't be true when she left Denville. The difference was she didn't have to cut Rhonda out of her life to move on. This time, she had a friend she planned to keep close. Even if it was from hundreds of miles away.

"I would love to be your maid of honor."

"Really?" Rhonda threw her arms around Claire. "The wedding is in October. I love fall."

Laughing, Claire hugged her friend.

October. The football season would be underway. Four or five games in. Logan would be starting for the Knights – Claire refused to believe otherwise – and she would be an assistant trainer. Again, she wouldn't let herself consider the alternative.

Getting a day off might be tricky. It was something she would worry about when the time came. Right now, she would order a blue dress and hope for the best. For Rhonda's wedding. For Logan's comeback. For her career.

With a small, silent whisper, she added – for a future with Logan.

CHAPTER ELEVEN

"Logan," the breathy voice said near his ear. "You look good enough to eat. Did you miss me?"

So close.

Logan sighed. Five more minutes, He would have paid for his groceries, been out the door, and on his way home. Instead, he had to deal with Linda Sue Hemmings. Luck had been his friend since that December night Claire walked into his life. He supposed he was due a couple of bumps.

If Linda Sue turned out to be the worst the fates had to throw at him, he would figure his luck held.

"Linda Sue."

Logan put the bran flakes back on the shelf before turning around. How had he missed that perfume? It was French – Linda Sue made sure everyone knew. If she doused on any more of it, the French would pick up the scent all the way from Oklahoma.

"What do you think?"

Linda Sue posed, one hand on her hip, the other moving toward Logan. Deftly, he sidestepped her attempt at contact. Nice move, Price. There wasn't a defensive lineman in the NFL as cagey as Linda Sue. If he could elude her grasp, he knew he was ready for Seattle.

"Nice…? Shirt?"

Logan hoped that was a satisfactory compliment. The sooner he figuratively gave Linda Sue a stroke, the sooner he could get home to Claire. This was their night off. Tuesdays were slow. His dad would close up after the last customer. If things held to form, midnight at the latest.

Logan's plans were all about Claire. Linda Sue was a pain in the ass he could do without.

"Silly," Linda Sue giggled. "I meant my tan. We just got back from Cozumel." She leaned closer, her whisper conspiratorial. "Hint. I'm brown *all* over."

Logan looked around, hoping no one witnessed Linda Sue's not so subtle maneuvers. He wasn't worried about word getting back to Claire. She wasn't the type to jump to unwarranted conclusions. Gossips could whisper all the trash they wanted, Claire would come to him for the truth. And he would tell it to her.

Logan worried about Linda Sue's husband. Darryl wasn't the brightest bulb – being trapped into marriage by this harpy was testimony to that. However, he didn't deserve to hear about his wife coming on to another man on the first day back in town.

Not that Darryl had anything to worry about from this quarter. Logan wanted one woman and one woman only. The overdressed, over-perfumed, over-made-up Linda Sue held no interest to him. He hadn't wanted her in high school or any of the times she had come on to him since he'd been back in Denville. He certainly didn't want her now.

He knew what it felt like to hold perfection. The thought of touching Linda Sue made Logan slightly sick to his stomach.

"Welcome, home. I have someplace to be, Linda Sue." Logan tried to push his cart toward the checkout aisle.

Undeterred, Linda Sue wrapped a hand around his arm, her long, red, lacquered nails biting through his shirt.

"I heard." Linda Sue's breath washed over his face. "Word has it you've gotten the lead back in your pencil. I'm sure your friend won't mind if you share a little of it with an old friend."

"The problem was never my lack of lead, Linda Sue. It was all about who was doing the sharpening."

Mouth agape, Linda Sue watched Logan get away – again. She wanted him. Had wanted him for as long as she could remember. The best-looking boy in Denville, she had assumed he would want to date the best-looking girl. She never understood why he wasn't interested.

When Logan's football career ended, Linda Sue knew that this time he would be hers. He had been thoroughly knocked off his high horse, and as before, she was the hottest woman around.

Nothing changed. Logan rebuffed her every come-on. His excuse?

She was a married woman. Linda Sue laughed. Nobody cared. Not even her husband. Darryl was so besotted, he let her do what she wanted with no repercussions.

She took one more glance Logan's way. She had been after him because he was the one that got away – her one defeat. Suddenly, she realized it was more than her ego. Linda Sue was in love. Or as close as she would ever get.

Without that scruffy beard and long hair, Logan looked like a movie star. She sighed. For him, she would consider having children. Imagine the beautiful babies they would produce. All he had to do was ask and she would leave safe old Darryl in a heartbeat.

Watching Logan leave the store without a backward glance, Linda Sue knew her dreams would never come true. She would never have Logan Price.

Her back went stiff when a plump, brassy redhead sauntered up to her. God, she hated this town. You couldn't turn around without someone being witness to your humiliation.

"Why do you keep putting yourself out there, girl? Logan Price has never been interested. Now that he's doing that blonde, he's even less likely to take what you're offering."

Charlene Thomas was Linda Sue's closest friend. They had been thick as thieves since the first grade. So she felt justified in eavesdropping from one aisle over. Now that Logan shot the other woman down, she rushed over to rub salt in a very old wound. After all, what were friends for?

"Who the hell is she?"

"Logan's piece of ass?" Charlene never pulled punches with her speech. Crude was her thing. "Some old girlfriend. She showed up just before Christmas and they've been going at it like rabbits ever since."

"Maybe she's his… what do you call it?" Linda Sue wracked her brain. "Beard. That's it."

Charlene laughed so hard she almost fell into the display of canned peas. "You think it's all for show? Honey, go into the bar some night. If those two aren't knocking boots on a regular basis, I'm a size two. And we both know I ain't ever been one of those."

Linda Sue's ears burned and her temper rose as she listened to Charlene cackle her way toward the bakery department. *Bitch*. Not just Charlene. It went for every woman she knew. Her so-called friends. Her mother-in-law.

Before she died, Linda Sue's mother qualified as the biggest bitch of all. Now, there was a new one. Claire Thornton.

Linda Sue felt the blood rushing to her face. She stomped her foot like a petulant child denied a bright, shiny toy that she had coveted for most of her life. How dare Logan refuse what she offered? How could he want someone else? Men in this town would jump through hoops to be with her.

Goddamn, Logan Price. Goddamn, his whore. The so-called love she had so graciously bestowed upon him just minutes earlier dissipated like a puff of smoke.

They would pay. Linda Sue didn't know when or how. She could wait. One day soon, she would find a way to make them both suffer.

"Hey, Linda Sue."

Rafer Macafee sauntered over, his stomach straining at the buttons on his flannel shirt. In one hand, he had a can of Copenhagen, in the other a bottle of cheap whiskey. The grin on his face said that he deluded himself with the idea that he still possessed the somewhat limited appeal he had in high school.

Linda Sue was about to set him straight when an idea percolated in her fevered brain. If there was one person in Denville who hated Logan more than she did, it was Rafer. She could use that.

Pushing out her considerable chest, Linda Sue gave Rafer her best fake smile. The man disgusted her, but she had slept with worse to get what she wanted. If she played this right, she might get Rafer to do her dirty work with only a few kisses and a promise of things to come. He always had been dumber than dirt.

"Hey, yourself," she purred. When Linda Sue saw the interest in Rafer's eyes intensify, she knew she had him. "You're just the man I was looking for."

"WHEN WAS THE last time you went dancing?"

"You mean on purpose?" Logan nuzzled Claire's ear.

They were sort of watching an old movie, though he had lost track of the plot after the first five minutes. Who cared what Fred and Ginger were up to when Claire was so close – smelling so damn good?

"Have you ever *accidentally* gone dancing?"

Claire tilted her head to allow Logan better access. She loved the feel of his lips. He had a knack for finding that one little spot that drove her crazy.

"Can't say that I have," Logan chuckled.

The vibration against her skin sent a lovely shiver through Claire's body.

"We should." She knew it wasn't a complete thought, but it was becoming more and more difficult for her to put together a sensible thought.

"Definitely." Logan's teeth closed over her lobe. "What should we do?"

I have no idea. Claire's hand drifted up Logan's thigh towards an interesting bulge between his legs that she wanted to check out.

"Dancing?"

"Hmm?"

"You want to go dancing?"

Why the hell would she want to go dancing when Logan's hand was up her shirt, teasing the slope of her breast? One more second and he would have it out of that pesky bra.

"I'm not big on it, but we can give it a go once we're back in Seattle."

"Logan." Claire took his face in her hands, her eyes meeting his. "Stop talking. Your mouth should be occupied doing crazy good things to my body. Now!"

"Bossy Claire is my favorite," Logan said with a wicked grin.

She was about to tell him where he could shove it when he did what she asked. He put his mouth on her body. Her lips, to be exact.

The kiss went from teasing to tempestuous in a heartbeat. By the time they came up for air, their clothes were strewn in every direction and they had equally satisfied smiles on their faces.

"I know I should get up." Claire snuggled closer. Logan's arms tightened around her.

"Why?"

"Because tomorrow is a big day. We need to get some sleep."

"Stress test," Logan sighed with resignation.

"Stress test," Claire said. She kissed his cheek. "Hey. We've done these from the very beginning and each time your knee is better. There's no reason to think this time will be any different."

Logan felt his gut clench. The stress test wasn't only on his knee – it was on his nerves. It never got any better. The only difference was he now knew what was coming. Or so he thought.

"Tomorrow, we're going all out."

"All out?" he asked with trepidation. "What does that mean?"

"You have to be able to make sudden sideways cuts." Claire made a zigzag motion with her hand. "Sometimes on grass, sometimes on turf. The test I've devised will give us a good idea how the knee will respond in a game situation."

"I could blow it out."

"I won't lie to you, Logan. There are no guarantees." Claire placed her hand on the leg that had been injured. "Every day, this gets stronger. But…"

"Athletes get injured. It happens."

There was a touch of resignation in his voice. Mostly, there was determination. It made Claire smile. Logan knew the odds were against him when they started this journey. Day by day. Month by month. The odds slowly began to tip in his favor.

Even though the human body was an amazing machine that could take a brutal amount of punishment, at times it could be as fragile as spun glass. A seemingly innocuous hit could end a career in a flash. Each individual was different. That was why some athletes played into their forties while others went out during their first training camp. You couldn't predict it. It wasn't fair.

No one knew that better than Logan.

"It's one day, Logan. One test."

"One foot in front of the other."

"One day at a time. Win one for the Gipper. Blah, blah, blah." When Logan smiled, Claire punched him in the arm. "You're going out there a nobody, but you've got to come back a star."

"Is that a sports cliché?" Logan asked with a frown.

"Nope. Straight from *42nd Street*." Grinning, Claire shrugged. "It worked for Ruby Keeler."

"I'll keep that in mind next time we're putting on a show in someone's barn."

"I'm so proud." Claire wiped away an imaginary tear. "You've learned much from me, Grasshopper. You may be the only NFL player to ever reference a Mickey Rooney musical."

Lying in bed an hour later, Logan chuckled again. Claire knew how to lighten a situation better than anyone he knew. She understood his anxiety. Knowing it did absolutely no good to dwell on something that was strictly a wait and see situation, she turned the conversation around until he was laughing his ass off. Her mind worked like a slightly off-kilter computer. She was so fast with her references that trying to keep up was a challenge. She was always one or two steps ahead of him, but he was starting to figure out how her thought processes worked. As a result, his mind was much more nimble. Fluid. One more thing that would be to his advantage if he made it back to the NFL.

Absently, Logan's hand moved to the empty side of the bed. Claire rarely stayed with him. It was the one thing about her that drove him crazy. He didn't ask – not anymore. It was always an awkward moment when she turned him down.

I've gotten used to sleeping alone.

My tossing and turning will keep you awake.

At least she had stopped using his father's delicate sensibilities as an excuse. That was lame from day one.

Logan hit his pillow, burrowing down with his back to the empty side of the bed. If the point of her sleeping by herself was to get him as much rest as possible, it was starting to backfire. Right now, he would take Claire any way he could get her. If she became too restless, he would hold her until she fell asleep.

Now didn't that sound good? Logan sighed. If slow and steady won the race back to professional football, it might work the same way with Claire. She liked having him in her life – there was no doubt about that. Getting her into his bed – all night – would come.

As his eyes grew heavy, his body relaxing into sleep, Logan wondered which was the bigger challenge. Getting his second chance? Or getting Claire?

"SO FAR SO good. This is the last obstacle, Logan. Up the hill, cut right, through the trees then down the embankment and back up the other side. When you hit the flat, book it back here as fast as you can."

"You're timing me?"

Claire held up the stopwatch. "Time is important, but I want you to concentrate on using both knees equally. Especially through that stand of Black Cypress. Like I said last night. Zig and zag. Like your life depends on it."

"Or my career," Logan said under his breath.

"Right." Claire was all business. The time for teasing was over. "You have to get used to going full-out, Logan. You aren't a promising rookie being given every chance. You're only getting this chance because Gaige used his influence."

"Gee, thanks." Logan closed his eyes, taking deep, calming breaths.

"Hey." Claire waited until Logan looked at her. Gripping him just below the shoulders, she held his gaze "The coaching staff will be looking for any excuse to cut you. We're going to make sure they can't find one." She gave his arms a reassuring squeeze. "Got it?"

"Got it."

Logan jumped up and down, shaking his arms. He was warmed up. They had been at this for over an hour.

With his father's help, Claire chose a spot for the tests well out of town, away from prying eyes. Normally, they would have started on the track at the high school. It would have been perfect for the stop and start drills. The hurdles, the practice dummies. All better suited than a rural field in the middle of nowhere.

Claire had given him the choice. Stay on the down low or go public. In the end, Logan decided he wasn't ready to face the inevitable questions. Soon, when the Knights released his name with a handful of other non-roster training camp invitees, he would have to deal with the media. That he could handle. Dealing with the residents of Denville was another matter.

"Ready?"

Logan stripped off his sweats. The late April sun was beating down like mid-July. Or maybe it was his imagination. Was his knee swelling? No. Claire would have noticed. It felt good. Strong.

"Ready."

Claire clicked the stopwatch. "Go."

Logan was halfway up the hill before Claire remembered to breathe. She tried to remove all personal feelings. Observe, record, report. Be a professional. Think of him as flesh and bone statistics. When Logan's foot slipped, his hand catching himself just before he tumbled to the ground, the air rushed out of her lungs in a rush. The second he reached the top, his healed knee pushing off toward the trees, Claire gave a silent cheer.

God, she was an idiot. This had stopped being strictly professional long ago. Up until five minutes ago, she had been fine with that. Then she started telling herself that if she could pretend she didn't have a personal stake in the outcome, she would be able to watch Logan run the course without stressing out.

With a shake of her head, Claire gripped the stopwatch, tossed her clipboard on the ground, and became one of the things she derided most in high school. A cheerleader.

"Go, Logan," she cried out at the top of her voice. "You're doing great. Hit the trees. That's it. Back and forth. Back and forth."

Again, Logan took it as though he was used to doing it every day and twice on Sunday. The sight of his sweat-covered face had Claire jumping in the air. Closer, closer.

When he crossed the finish, Claire did what any professional would do. She hit the stop button on the watch.

When he kept coming toward her, she did what any woman with half a brain would do. She screamed with happiness and jumped into his arms.

"How's the knee?" Claire asked, peppering his sweaty face with kisses.

"Good," he laughed.

Logan was physically worn out. Emotionally spent. *Done*. Keeping one arm around Claire's waist, he fell onto a patch of soft green grass. He made sure she landed on top of him. Then, switching positions, his mouth landed on hers.

Claire kissed him back, her legs tangling with his.

"I should check your knee."

"Feels as loose as I do." Logan slid his hand under her t-shirt, humming with pleasure when he reached her breast.

"Where are you finding the energy?"

"Unknown reserves. Mmm." His sigh told Claire how much he enjoyed her roving mouth.

"You taste like a salt-lick. Drink some water, and then let me examine your knee."

When Claire tried to wiggle out from under him, Logan used his free hand to trap her wrists above her head.

"Later." He took her mouth again. When he pulled away, they were *both* breathing hard. "I've conquered my Mt. Everest, Claire. I choose to celebrate by enjoying your delectable body. Do you have a problem with that?"

At that moment, Logan looked so happy; she wouldn't have denied him a thing. Two hundred pounds of sweaty, sexy male. Yum. Blue eyes sparkling, Claire smiled.

"Who am I to argue with Oklahoma's answer to Edmund Hillary? Celebrate away."

Logan and Claire tore at each other's clothes, blissfully unaware of the man who watched from a stand of trees less than thirty feet away.

When he followed Price and his piece of ass out of town, Rafer Macafee had been certain it was a waste of time. He figured he would take a few pictures, show them to Linda Sue to prove he followed her instructions, and then receive his reward. The bitch had been teasing him since high school.

Agreeing to spy on Price for a few hours was worth it if it meant finally dipping his dick into Linda Sue. She was so damn smug. Rafer wasn't as stupid as people thought. He knew she planned to welch on her end of the bargain. She would bat her eyes like when they were teenagers. That used to dazzle him. He would give her whatever money he had without asking for anything in return. She was crazy enough to think she could still get away with that shit. Well, not this time.

Bored out of his skull, Rafer watched, at first not understanding what he was seeing. However, after a while, a light clicked on.

Son of a bitch. Those weren't regular exercises. They were modified football drills. There was only one reason for Logan Price to be out here, away from prying eyes, doing that. He was going to try for a comeback.

Rafer felt a familiar surge of envy. For as long as he could remember, he wanted Logan's life. Logan was taller. Faster. Stronger. All the girls wanted Logan. While he got the homecoming queen, Rafer ended up with the head of the decorating committee. Price got a fancy scholarship while Rafer went to work at his father-in-law's feed and seed.

Rafer never saw the hard work Logan put in – the sacrifices. He knew one thing. Logan always got what he wanted.

Now, the cocksucker was going for it again.

Rafer watched, sneering as Logan made love to Claire. *What a pussy.* The bitch was obviously in heat, but instead of ramming his dick home, the asshole took it slow. Romantic shit.

Not bothering to stay to the end, Rafer made his way back to where he had parked his truck. Inside the cab, he pounded his fists on the steering wheel. No! Not this time. He wasn't going to stand by while Logan Price once again became Denville's golden boy.

Starting the engine, Rafer put the truck in gear, turning toward town. He had to think of a way to stop this. His brain searched for the answer. Wait. That was it. Grinning, he pulled out his phone.

"Linda Sue? Have I got something to tell you."

CHAPTER TWELVE

"COME ON, PUG. Admit it. Rhonda has you so far wrapped around her finger you'll never get free."

"Why would I want to?"

It was asked with such simple sincerity that none of the men at the table had the heart to continue teasing the big man. Though none would admit it, one or two of them envied having a woman to feel that way about.

Stanley *Pug* Doughty was well liked in Denville. He was born there, grew up, and became Deputy Sheriff. He had traveled a bit. After high school, he spent two years seeing the United States. He worked on a fishing boat in Alaska. The oil fields in Texas. He even worked as a bodyguard in New York City.

Pug wasn't born with wanderlust. It was either get out of town or go crazy watching the only woman he had ever loved throw her life away on a no-good sack of shit. He couldn't save a woman who didn't know she needed saving. He had spent too long eating his heart out over Rhonda Sykes.

So Pug got out of Denville. If asked, he would say the time away did him good – seasoned him. It turned out he was a simple Oklahoma boy. After a while, he knew it was time to come back home.

Any hope that his time away had cured his love for Rhonda was shot down the second he saw her. Resigned, Pug knew he was going to spend his life alone. His heart belonged to a curvy brunette with a touch of the devil in her smile. He couldn't marry another woman. It wouldn't be fair. No matter how hard he tried, no one compared to Rhonda.

Becoming a police officer had always been his dream. He studied hard. Worked his ass off. He decided to be the best damn cop Denville had ever known. Now, years later he was living the dream. He had the whole package. A job he loved in the town it was his honor to serve and protect.

As for his personal life? Someone was watching out for Stanley *Pug* Dougherty because that was as close to perfect as it could get. Rhonda Sykes – the only woman he would ever love – was his. Heart, soul, and two great kids to boot. Let his friends rib him. That was fine with Pug. Rhonda *did* have him wrapped around her finger. And he loved every second of it.

"Are the Neanderthals giving you a hard time, sweetheart?"

Rhonda, tray at her side, put her arm around Pug's shoulder. She squeezed him hard, loving the feel of him. Big, solid, dependable Pug. He might not be the first man she had loved, but he was by far the best. The best and the last.

"Nothing I can't handle, Rhonda."

Pug always called her Rhonda. Not baby. Not honey. Rhonda. He said it with love. With a touch of reverence tossed in. The way he said it made her feel warm all over. Protected.

There was never any worry that Rhonda would take Pug for granted. After years of dealing with her ex-husband, she knew how lucky she was. Pug was hers and she was never letting go.

"Well, they better watch it. I'm keeping my eyes on you guys." Rhonda gave the table of policemen a wink. "Treat him right."

"Or?" Lyle Jaffe, Pug's best friend, challenged her with a smile.

Rhonda smiled back, but her eyes were deadly serious. "I'll kick your ass."

The men whooped with laughter. Only Pug knew she was serious. Rhonda protected those she thought of as hers. His chest puffed up with happiness. Now, that small, exclusive group included him.

"Another round of beer for Pug's table," Rhonda called out to Logan when she got back to the bar. "On me."

"That looks like the entire police department," Logan observed, filling a frost-covered pitcher. "Who's minding the town?"

"A couple of them are from over in Masters." Getting rid of the old ones, Rhonda added fresh glasses to her tray. "This is an unofficial pre-bachelor party."

"Is that even a thing?" Logan laughed. He handed her a bowl of peanuts.

"It is now."

"What?" Logan asked. Rhonda stared at him with a slightly bemused expression.

"You're so damn good looking," she exclaimed.

"Rhonda." Logan shook his head. "It's been a few days since I lost the beard. Besides, you knew what I looked like before."

"I was used to seeing you one of two ways. The mountain man or the boy I knew in high school." Rhonda turned her head back and forth, considering him from every angle. "Under all that hair was a new man. You were always pretty."

"Well, shit," Logan muttered.

Rhonda laughed. "Bear with me. You aren't pretty anymore."

"Thank you."

"You're... seasoned."

"As in liberally doused with salt and pepper?"

"Ha, ha," Rhonda snickered. "You should consider taking that act on the road. I meant as you've gotten older, you've lost that soft look. Now, you're yummy."

"Are you flirting with my girl?"

"Other way around, deputy." Logan held out his hand, gripping Pug's. "She never could leave me alone."

"In your dreams." Rhonda leaned into Pug, her dark head resting just below his chin.

"Logan has his own dream girl, Rhonda. You're all mine."

"Yes," Rhonda sighed. "I am."

Logan smiled at the couple. The freckled good old boy and the ex-cheerleader. They were an unlikely couple who fit together perfectly.

"She's too good for you," Logan said.

"No."

"Absolutely."

Pug and Rhonda spoke the words simultaneously, causing everyone within earshot to laugh.

"Take it from an old married couple. That attitude is going to take you a long way."

"Are you and Trina blessing our future union?"

Ron Watkins and his wife Trina came into *Lefty's Pub* once a week, every week. Thirty years and running. Like clockwork. They sat at the same table. Ordered the same drinks. Whiskey and soda for him. A screwdriver for her. They stayed for an hour. Sometimes two, if friends were around. Their one drink apiece lasted them until they left for home.

In good weather, they walked from their home four blocks away, then back again. When it rained or snowed, Trina drove them the short distance in their old Buick.

Their fifty-year marriage was the sturdiest thing in Denville. Solid. Bedrock. If Ron approved of Rhonda and Pug, the chances were good that they would last to their own golden anniversary.

"Do you *need* my blessing?"

"No," Rhonda said. "But I would like it."

As he always did, Ron looked at Trina before he answered. An old habit that was another secret to their long, happy union. Never take the other person for granted.

Trina didn't say anything. She didn't have to. Ron could read her thoughts in her sweet, brown eyes. He lifted her hand to his lips. Every heart in the bar, women and men, sighed.

"You have our blessing and more."

"More?" Rhonda and Pug exchanged interested glances.

"A dance with the bride and groom. At your wedding. Think of it as this old, happy couple passing the torch."

"I think I'm going to cry." Rhonda rushed over, giving Ron and Trina a hug.

"I'm feeling a little choked up myself," Pug whispered to Logan.

"Right there with you, buddy." Logan slapped Pug on the back.

"I have decided they are officially my favorite married people." Claire joined Logan behind the bar.

"Where have you been?" Logan asked. He draped an arm over Claire's shoulder, kissing her temple.

"To put it delicately, I needed to go to the ladies' room."

"Since when are you delicate?"

"Thanks a lot." Claire dug her elbow into Logan's side.

"Hey, I like strong, bruising types." Rubbing his ribs, Logan grinned at Pug over Claire's head. "Arms like steel, Pug."

"Brains like mush, Pug." Claire tapped Logan's head with the finger before moving away.

"Now you've done it." Pug watched as Claire pulled Rhonda aside. "You've pissed her off."

"Nope." Logan knew his woman. "That's our form of foreplay. Just watch. In a few minutes, she'll be pulling me into the back room. The woman can't keep her hands off me."

"Jesus, Logan." Pug shook his head in amazement. "Do you really talk to her like that? And Claire likes it?"

"We understand each other." Logan felt the now familiar warmth spread through him when he thought about how well she suited him. "Have you ever seen *The Awful Truth*? Or *My Man Godfrey*?"

"Never heard of them."

"Banter. Fast and furious, my friend." Claire and her movies. It seemed they were seeping into his brain whether he liked it or not. Unstoppable osmosis. "Every now and then, we become Cary Grant and Irene Dunne."

"Whatever works." Pug had no idea what Logan was talking about, but he seemed happy. In the end, that was all that mattered.

"Enter the world's biggest buzz kill."

Hearing Logan's mumbled comment, Pug looked over his shoulder. Rafer Macafee and his cronies stumbled through the door.

"Looks like they started drinking before they got here," he said, frowning.

"Which means I can refuse to serve them, right?"

"Legally, it's the only way to go."

"Well, Deputy, it sounds like the law knows what it's doing."

Practically rubbing his hands together in anticipation, Logan started over. Better to let the idiots know how things stood before they entrenched themselves at a table.

"Why don't you let me handle it, Logan?" Pug nodded toward his friends. "I have plenty of backup if they get rowdy."

"You want to deprive me of my fun?"

"Logan—"

Logan gave Pug a reassuring look. "I promise. I won't be the instigator."

Pug shook his head. Logan knew damn well when it came to Rafer Macafee, his mere presence set the other man off. Quickly, he circled the room, stopping by Rhonda and Claire.

"Stay out of the way."

"What way? What are you talking about?" Rhonda demanded when Pug kept moving. Rhonda scanned the room. "Oh, crap."

"What?" Claire asked.

"Logan and Rafer." Rhonda sighed. "Or as we used to call them in high school, Beauty and the Beast."

"Logan must have loved that." Claire kept her eyes on the other side of the bar, ready to jump in. Logan could handle himself. However, one against five? She didn't like the odds.

"Logan never knew. Rafer found out, though." Rhonda shuddered. "He beat up the poor guy who was stupid enough to tell him to his face. And when I say beat up? Cory Dodd lost two teeth and limped for a month."

"Was he arrested?"

"Nope."

"Are you kidding?" Claire's eyes blazed blue fire. Outraged didn't begin to describe how she felt.

"Cory wouldn't tell his parents or the police who was responsible."

"So the psycho got away with it."

"I didn't say that."

Still watching as Logan blocked Rafer from sitting down, Claire said, "Spit it out, Rhonda. What happened?"

"Logan." Rhonda grinned at the memory. "He never knew what set Rafer off. He did know that Rafer outweighed Cory by over a hundred pounds. Justice was swift and brutal at Denville High. At the next football practice, Rafer ended up on the bottom of every pile."

"Ouch." Claire said it with a grin.

"He was punched, kicked, gouged. If you were next to Rafer, you took your shot. Coach Bradshaw had no idea anything was going on until Rafer crawled off the field."

"Did Rafer squeal?"

"No." Rhonda shook her head. "I'll bet he wanted to. I guess he wanted to stay on the team more. If he had said anything, the other guys would have made that impossible."

Claire felt a rush of unease. When a man hated him that much for so long, there was no telling what might happen.

It seemed that everyone in the room was aware of Logan and Rafer. Pug's friends looked ready to intervene at a moment's notice. The bar wasn't silent, but the noise level had definitely diminished.

Some of the patrons hoped for a fight – what better way to liven up a dull evening in Denville? Others, like Claire and Rhonda, hoped that Logan wouldn't prod his old nemesis too hard and that Rafer would for once be the bigger man. By the set of their shoulders, it didn't seem like either was going to back down.

"Well, I'll be damned," Rhonda breathed.

"Rafer is leaving? Just like that?" Claire glanced at Rhonda.

"Miracles do happen. Now I'm waiting for the pigs to fly by."

Logan waited until the last of Rafer's crowd had left the bar. He was as surprised as everyone else. In all the years he had known Rafer Macafee, he couldn't recall a single conversation that hadn't been a war of wills. Tension crackled in the air. Insults flew. The hatred was palpable. Never once had Rafer walked away without at least a verbal confrontation.

"What happened?" Pug asked.

Logan kept his eyes on the door, expecting Rafer to suddenly change his mind. After a solid minute, he finally gave in to the fact that for once, there would be no blowback.

It was a relief – mostly. Twisted as it might be, a little part of Logan would always enjoy a possible brush-up with Rafer. Call it part of the Denville experience. Every small town had its bully. Putting him in his place was satisfying on so many levels.

"He'll be back," Pug reassured Logan. "Next time, he'll be twice as ornery."

"Am I that obvious?" Logan had the good grace to look embarrassed. Enjoying Rafer's idiocy was supposed to be his dirty little secret. Apparently, the secret part was only in his mind.

"I've watched the two of you go at it for most of my life. I know you could live without the drama."

"But it does spice things up."

"As long as nobody ends up with worse than the occasional split lip, what's the harm?"

"What's the harm?" Rhonda demanded. "Pug, I thought you were sworn to uphold the peace. Now I hear you encouraging Logan?"

"Rhonda…"

"Do you ever wish there was an alternative to men?" Rhonda asked Claire. "At this moment, I would cheerfully become a lesbian."

"Cheerfully?" Claire understood the sentiment. However, when one loved the feel of a man's body over hers, it was hard to give it up – no matter how annoying he could be.

"I think you're hot." Rhonda looked Claire up and down, then sighed. "Oh, who am I kidding? I like men. I *love* this one. When it comes to my sex life, I guess it will always be dicks before chicks. Sorry, Claire."

"Maybe in another life," Claire chuckled. The smile left her face when her gaze met Logan's. "I don't know what to say."

"This is Oklahoma."

"What the hell does that mean?" Claire threw up her hands. "Not everyone who lives in the state is one brain cell away from an asylum. Doesn't Trisha Yearwood live in Oklahoma?"

"Trisha Yearwood?" Logan looked to Pug for help. The other man wisely refrained from commenting.

"Come on, Rhonda. The testosterone in the air is giving me a headache."

"First fight?" Pug asked.

"Was that a fight? Claire has yelled at me. Punched me in the arm. One time, I barely missed being beaned by a tennis shoe. Those things I could understand. I've never seen Claire so… irrational."

"Shh," Pug lowered his voice. "Never say that about a woman when she's within hearing distance. That is one of the words guaranteed to have you doing without for at least a week."

"Really?" Logan didn't like the sound of that. "What are the other words?"

Pug laughed. "Hell if I know. With Rhonda, it's a crapshoot. I think the last one that set her off was *girl*. As in *did you just call me a girl?*"

"She isn't a girl?"

"Woman, my friend. Stick with woman. Claire might not be as sensitive about that as Rhonda, but why chance it?"

Logan felt like he had been dumped into a foreign world where he no longer understood the language or the customs. Girl? Woman? He had known Claire since December. Four intense, emotional months. They worked together. Shared their meals. Played. Made love.

If they had met under normal circumstance and started dating, how long would it take to know her the way he did now? A year? Two? It had been a crash course in Claire – Logan, the enthusiastic student.

There were plenty of mysteries left to discover. Up until now, Logan hadn't worried about words that would trigger potential blow-ups. Why start? He wanted to discover everything he could about Claire. Hopefully, it would take the rest of their lives.

"Looks like Claire wants to see you."

Looking over his shoulder, Logan saw Claire pointing toward the office. He nodded.

"I'll see you later, Pug."

"Hey, Dad," Logan called out to his father who was manning the far end of the bar. "Can you take it solo for a few minutes?"

Jonas gave Logan a thumb's up.

"Claire?" Logan called out.

The office was dark. He flipped the light switch. Seeing her standing across the room, her back to him, Logan frowned. What was wrong?

"Are we fighting?" Even if he didn't know the reason, Logan wanted to at least be in the loop.

"I feel like a fool."

"Okay." Logan approached her, his arms sliding around her waist. "That happens so seldom. Want to share?"

"You can take care of yourself."

"Most of the time."

"You've dealt with Rafer for years."

"More than I care to remember."

Claire turned in his arms. She wasn't crying, but Logan could see a trace of moisture in her eyes.

"I've never worried about anyone the way I worry about you." Claire shook her head. "No. Strike that. Worry isn't the right word. I care what happens to you."

Logan felt his heart skitter. *Care* wasn't love, but he'd take it. For now.

"I care about you, too."

"I've been flying solo for so long, Logan. I have friends. Gaige is a big part of my life."

"But…?"

"They all come and go." Claire rested her head on Logan's chest. The faint beat of his heart was reassuring to her oddly frazzled nerves. "I've gotten used to spending most of my time alone. I like it that way."

"I crashed into your solitary life." Logan smoothed back her long, bright, blond hair. So soft. He breathed deeply. Lemons. He loved the way she always smelled fresh and clean.

"You weren't supposed to be anything but a job, Logan. A means to an end. The next step."

"I won't say I'm sorry, Claire." Logan put a finger under her chin, tilting it to look into her eyes. "Do you regret coming here? Are you sorry I've come to mean more to you than another rung in what's been a very long ladder?"

"So long." Claire sighed. "I'm not sorry, Logan. That said, I don't know if I know how to do this – us – once we're back in Seattle."

"Do you want to try?"

Logan held his breath.

"Yes, but—"

"Stop right there." Logan kissed her parted lips. Mmm. So damn sweet. "Yes. I like that. I can work with yes."

"You can, huh?" Claire smiled. "You think I'm worth the trouble?"

Logan threaded his fingers through her hair. "You're the best kind of trouble I've ever known, Claire. Why wouldn't I want to take a chance?"

Claire knew she should have a logical answer to that. However, Logan's kiss made arguing seem like a waste of time when she could be enjoying the feel of his lips against hers. They would have plenty of time to figure this out.

Claire wrapped her arms around Logan, sinking into his heat. Hot kisses. Sexy man. A man she grew closer to every day.

"That couch looks awfully inviting," Logan whispered.

"You father will figure out what we're doing."

"My father and everyone else."

"That doesn't bother you?"

"Nope," Logan said. "But I know it bothers you." Taking her hand, he started toward the door. "Later?"

Claire squeezed his hand. "You can count on it."

"Oh, I am."

Logan counted on a whole lot more. Claire would see how good they could be. Not just here in Oklahoma. Back in Seattle. Anywhere. They worked. Together.

IT TURNED OUT to be one of those lingering crowds.

The mood turned mellow and friendly. Ron and Trina stayed later than usual. The jukebox played some old favorites. Fast for toe tapping. Slow for dancing.

Rhonda and Pug took advantage of the moment. They got their wedding dance with Ron and Trina early. Logan smiled. Watching the older couple give a master course on gliding across the floor in another person's arms.

"They are amazing."

Claire set the tray of dirty glasses by the sink. Logan drew her close. He rested his cheek on her hair.

"Want to take a spin?"

"This isn't the first time you've offered to take me dancing. Is there a frustrated Fred Astaire in there trying to get out?"

"No." Logan laughed. "I like the idea of holding you in my arms. In private. In public. Any place."

"Why, Logan Price. You are a romantic!"

"Would it be too corny to say you bring it out in me?'

"Maybe." Claire pretended to consider her answer. "Nope. I'll take all the romance I can get. As long as it's from you."

"Oh, good. We can be corny together."

It was almost an hour later when Logan locked the door.

"That was so much fun," Rhonda sighed. "But my feet are killing me. Note to self. Change shoes at the reception. I'm not dancing the night away in the four-inch stilettos I bought to walk down the aisle."

"Why do you need that high of a heel?" Pug asked. He stuck around to drive Rhonda home. In the meantime, he helped her bus tables. "Who is going to see them under your dress?"

Tugging on his ear, Rhonda pulled Pug down to her level. "I love that you're tall, sweetheart, but I don't want all the pictures to either have your head or mine. Four inches should just about lift me to an acceptable photograph level."

"Who knew there was so much to think about?" Pug grinned. "Should I be doing more?"

"All you have to do is show up. That's the most important thing of all."

"While you two make googley eyes, I'm going to take these empties out to the recycle bin. The pick-up is tomorrow morning. I don't want to miss it again."

"Sorry, boss," Rhonda called out. "I'm not used to Denville joining the twentieth century. Those trucks are still a shock to the system."

"Yah, yah, yah," Logan muttered good-naturedly.

"Need some help?" Claire called out.

"Stay and enjoy your coffee. I'm good."

Claire watched Logan back his way out the side door, two big rattling bags in his hands. An unexpected shiver ran down her spine.

"Is something wrong?" Jonas asked from across the bar.

"I don't know. I just feel… something."

Unable to let it go, Claire slipped off the stool. If she met Logan on his way back, fine. No harm done. However, if something was wrong, she didn't want to wait around to find out.

LOGAN FROWNED WHEN he noticed the broken outdoor light over the door. It wasn't like that a few hours ago. Probably some kids getting their kicks. He made a mental note to replace it as soon as he got to work tomorrow.

As Logan hefted the bags of bottles into the bin, he caught movement out of the corner of his eye. That one flash of warning was all that saved him from a baseball bat to the knee.

Jumping to his right, Logan hit the ground and rolled. A loud thud from the bag hitting the hard plastic bin was followed by a string of curse words.

"Goddamned slippery bastard. Stand still." Rafer took another swing, this one so wild it almost took out the two men standing next to him. Logan didn't take the time to identify Rafer's cohorts. He assumed they were part of the same group that always ran together. All that mattered was that this wasn't going to be a fair fight. Rafer, a Louisville Slugger and at least… one, two others. Logan wasn't going to stick around to find out how many he could take down before *they* downed *him*.

"He's heading for the door. Stop him, Wade."

Wade Eaton. Another ex-football player at Denville High. Back then, they took sides. Pro-Rafer. Pro-Logan. All these years later, nothing had changed. Except Rafer's friends spent their free time swilling beer and eating anything fried. By himself, one was no match for Logan's speed. He was around Wade before the other man could do more than shift his bulk a few meager feet.

Unfortunately, the other two men were already in place at the door. They moved out of the shadows just as Logan reached for the knob. He might have fought them off. However, before he could throw a punch, he was cold-cocked by a two-by-four. Flat on his back, his head rang like the bells of Notre Dame, Logan tried to gather his sense. *Stand up. Fight.*

He opened his eyes. In front of him were two Rafers, neither of them very clear. There was one thing Logan couldn't miss, blurry eyes or not. A baseball bat raised and ready to strike.

When Logan tried to roll out of range, he was grabbed by each arm. Wade and Mason Blaylock. Shit. The man was a mountain. In high school, he was league defensive player of the year. Logan was in better shape, but between them, Wade and Mason outweighed him by at least two hundred pounds. It took some effort, but with the aid of their superior size, they managed to hold him down.

"Think you're going back to the NFL?" Rafer sneered. He tapped the wooden bat against his hand. "Well, think again."

Bracing for the pain of impact, Logan knew this was it. There would be no recovering this time. His dreams and Claire's were over.

THE SECOND CLAIRE opened the door she knew exactly what was happening.

The men holding Logan. The blood running down the side of his face. Rafer Macafee raising a bat with the intent of shattering Logan's knee. There was no time to get help. No time to think things through. She did the only thing she could.

She raised the gun and fired.

CHAPTER THIRTEEN

"**Y**OU FUCKING BITCH. You shot me."

Rafer screamed the words from a writhing heap on the ground.

"Damn straight. Do something smart for the first time in your life. Stay down or I'll shoot you again." Claire held the gun firmly, her hands steady as a rock. The rest of her was a mess.

"Logan? Are you all right? Answer me, or I'm going to shoot Rafer again."

"Hey," Rafer protested.

"Shut up. You two," Claire swung the gun toward the men who had been holding Logan down. "Not another step."

Stunned by the turn of events, it had taken them a few moments to react. The alcohol that had given them the courage to follow Rafer's crazy plan was wearing off. Self-preservation mode kicked in. However, they weren't fast enough. Claire pinned them down before they could scamper off to their holes like the rats that they were. They could have made a break for it. However, they were just sober enough to play it smart. If it was a choice between jail and bleeding, they chose jail.

"Logan!" Claire called again, her voice sharp with worry.

"I'm fine. I wanted to see if you would really shoot that bastard again."

"I'm bleeding to death."

"Shut up," Claire and Logan shouted simultaneously.

"What the hell happened?"

Pug came running from the bar. Rhonda and Jonas were right behind.

"Take this. And don't let anyone get away." Claire shoved the gun at Pug.

"Is that mine?" Rhonda asked, her eyes wide as she looked around the parking lot.

Claire didn't pause to explain how she had grabbed the weapon out of Rhonda's purse before coming outside. In an instant, she was at Logan's side. She ran her hands up and down his leg, checking for an injury.

"Where did he get you?" she demanded.

"In the head. Though it wasn't Rafer who knocked me down." Logan lifted a hand to his head, wincing. "My leg is fine, Claire. Claire," Logan sat up, taking her hands in his. "He didn't touch my leg. I promise."

"Oh my God. Oh my God." Claire threw herself into Logan's arms. When she heard his hiss of pain, she pulled back instantly. "We need to get you to the hospital. You might have a concussion."

"No."

"No?" Claire exclaimed. "You're going to the hospital if I have to carry you myself."

"Claire."

Without another word, Logan gently gathered her close. She was shaking. A natural reaction, all things considered. He held on, swaying slightly until she began to settle. Around them, things were in a state of chaos. Pug held the gun in one hand while he called for backup with the other.

Jonas quickly assessed the situation. His first concern was Logan. Once he realized his son would be all right, he quickly went to the ice machine, retrieved his gun, and returned to the parking lot.

Pug didn't say anything. He gave Jonas a long, considering look. Deciding he wasn't in rabid vigilante mode, Pug nodded. It would be a few minutes until the police arrived. Having another set of eyes, not to mention another gun, could only help.

Rhonda, weapon-free, knelt by the still groaning Rafer. Cool as a cucumber, she took the bar towel from the waistband of her apron. With the skill of a mother with two young, active children, she wrapped the cloth around his arm.

"Here," Rhonda grabbed Rafer's other hand. "Hold this down and keep a steady pressure. Oh, stop your caterwauling. It's only a flesh wound."

"I've lost a lot of blood," Rafer cried out pitifully.

"And you'll lose more if you don't keep that towel in place." Rhonda rolled her eyes in disgust. "You're lucky I'm helping you at all. If I weren't worried that there was a slight chance you might die, I wouldn't bother."

"You care if he dies?" Pug asked when Rhonda joined him.

"No. But Claire might. Shooting someone is hard enough. She doesn't need to have the burden of taking someone's life. Even scum like Rafer."

"I wouldn't lose any sleep over it," Claire called out, her voice muffled against Logan's chest.

"Sure you would," Logan whispered for her ears only. "My warrior woman might be tough as nails, but she has a soft heart. Even for scum like Rafer Macafee."

"Shh. I don't want that getting around."

Logan closed his eyes, the pounding in his head lessening with the feel of Claire in his arms. He knew she was only half-joking. Claire was strong. Inside and out. He knew she liked to project an *I don't give a shit* attitude. He knew for the most part that was true.

He also knew there were a select few things that Claire Thornton cared about deeply. Her work. Her friends. And more and more, Logan was convinced she cared about him. Not just as a rehabilitation project. Or a lover. She might not be ready to admit it – but he was in her heart.

The sounds of sirens signaled the approach of the police. The ambulance arrived at the same time.

"Jesus," Logan groused when one of the EMTs ran a little flashlight in front of his eyes. "I told you, I'm fine."

"And I told you, you're getting checked out," Claire said firmly. "It's either here or in the hospital."

"Fine," Logan sighed. He hated hospitals. He shut his mouth and let the man do his job.

Rafer wasn't keeping quiet. He had been shot! That bitch was not getting away with it.

"I want to press charges," he shouted. The woman dressing his arm winced.

"Shut up and let me do my job. We'll get you to the hospital, and then you can talk to the police."

"I'll do more than talk." Rafer didn't lower his voice. He got louder. "I have witnesses. That crazy cunt shot me for no reason."

"Is he serious?" Claire asked in amazement. "And did he call me a cunt?"

"After everything that's happened, *that* is what bothers you?" Logan chuckled.

"Everything about that idiot bothers me," Claire assured Logan.

"I know people." Rafer continued his rant as he was wheeled to the ambulance. "My father-in-law has money. You'll pay for this. All of you will pay."

"Your father-in-law will happily let you rot in jail," Rhonda called out.

"My advice is to come in for further tests," the EMT officer said. He finished cleaning the cut on Logan's head and applied a bandage. Stitches weren't necessary. "I don't think you have a concussion."

"I told you," Logan said to Claire.

"However," the man continued. "Better safe than sorry."

"Please, Logan." Claire squeezed his hand. "You can't fool around with a head injury. There could be internal bleeding."

Logan could have held out against anything but the concern in Claire's blue eyes. Causing her worry was the last thing he wanted. Even if it meant a trip to the dreaded hospital.

"Fine. But I'm not riding with Rafer."

"I'll drive you," Claire smiled with relief. She turned to Pug, who was conferring with a uniformed officer. "Am I under arrest?"

"Very funny." Pug shook his head. "Since I know where to find you, you can go. Come to the police station tomorrow and give your statement."

"Will do. Thanks, Pug." Claire helped Logan to his feet. "Do you want to come, Jonas?"

"Are you okay, Logan?"

"You know how hard my head is, Dad."

Jonas nodded. Inside, he was still a quivering mass of worry. He hadn't seen what went down, but he knew it was bad. Football be damned, this time, Logan might not have walked away. Literally. Rafer might have crippled Logan for life. Or, Jonas shuddered at the thought, killed him. Seeing his son strong. Standing. He said a silent thank you.

"He's a lousy patient, Claire." Jonas kept his tone light. "You deal with him. I'll stay here and close up the bar."

Claire carefully helped Logan into the cab of his old pickup truck.

"I can buckle my own seatbelt, Claire."

"Quiet." She kissed him on the cheek. "Let me fuss, okay?"

"Will that make you feel better?"

"Probably."

Claire met Logan's gaze. The dried blood on his face and the memory of him flat on his back with Rafer about to crush his kneecap were the only things that kept her from smacking the little smirk off his face.

"You like that I was worried sick?"

"I like that you were worried," Logan amended. "I like that you care."

"Of course I care." Claire's eyes widened. "Were there any doubts?"

"No." Only to what degree. Logan kept that caveat to himself. "Fuss away, Claire."

"Screw you, Logan."

Claire tried to slam the door. With one hand, Logan blocked her; with the other, he pulled her close.

"Claire." Logan spoke her name as a soft caress. "Claire. Please. I need you to make a fuss."

For the first time, Claire heard the vulnerability in Logan's voice. The adrenaline was wearing off. The reality of what almost happened had sunk in. This time, Logan started shaking.

"I've got you." Claire wrapped him in her arms. "I'm not letting go."

Silently she added – not now, not ever.

IT TURNED OUT Logan was right. He had a hard head.

After running a series of tests, including a CAT scan, Logan's doctor proclaimed him concussion-free.

"If you experience lingering headaches past tomorrow, come back right away," Dr. Samuels told Logan. He insisted Claire be in the room. Logan wanted her to hear it from a professional. "Other than that, I'd say you were lucky. Keep the bandage in place and dry for another few days. There shouldn't even be a scar."

"Thank you, Dr. Samuels." Logan shook the man's hand.

"Don't say it," Claire as she turned the truck onto the highway.

"What?"

"This is not an *I told you so* moment."

"Well…" Logan rubbed his chin thoughtfully, tapping his mouth with one finger. "I seem to recall telling you the hospital was a waste of time and money.

Claire gave Logan a quick glance. He looked like exactly what he was. A man who had survived a nasty attack. His hair stuck out in several odd directions, part of it matted with dried blood. On his forehead, around the edges of the bandage, a dark bruise was forming. From the looks of it, it was going to be a doozy.

Logan's clothes were streaked with dirt, sweat, and blood. Some of it was his. The splatters on the lower half of his jeans belonged to Rafer. He was tired, beaten, bruised, and bloody. And with all that, Logan Price still sent her heart beating a mile a minute.

There was no figuring out why one person revved his motor. Or why the next person didn't. At his worst, Logan was still the sexiest man she had ever known.

"You can say you told me so," Claire reached for Logan's hand. "I would make the same call every time. Understand?"

Logan raised her fingers to his lips. One by one, he kissed them. When he reached her thumb, he lightly bit down.

"Understood."

"And Logan?"

"Hmm?"

"Try not to put either of us in that position – ever again."

Keeping her hand in his, Logan rested his head against the seat. He closed his eyes.

"I'll try my best." He waited for a beat. "But no guarantees."

When he heard Claire grumble under her breath, Logan chuckled. It felt good to tease her. It felt good to be here. In one piece. On his way home.

Claire was making a habit of saving him.

She had pulled him out of his depression. Given him that spark of hope. Bit by bit, she strengthened his body along with his resolve.

Tonight she stopped an attack that might have ended any chance of a comeback. In all likelihood, it would have crippled him for life.

Claire Thornton had given him everything. Would she be able to give him one more thing? Her heart?

The thought swirled in Logan's head as he drifted off to sleep, making him smile. When had he become such a greedy bugger? He wanted it all. A career with the Knights. Fame. Fortune. And the most important thing of all. Claire.

Was that asking for too much? Logan didn't care. This time? No matter what, he planned to get it all.

CHAPTER FOURTEEN

LOGAN RECOVERED NICELY from the knock on his head by letting Claire take over. Not that it was any hardship.

Hot soup. Aspirin. Plenty of TLC. All served up by a beautiful woman with a body that was made to drool over and a smile that could stop traffic on the autobahn.

A man would have to be crazy not to revel in that kind of attention. Logan was many things – crazy wasn't one of them.

His only complaint was Claire's temporary moratorium on sex.

When they got home the night of Rafer's attack, Logan took a quick shower, making sure to keep his head wound away from the spray of water. Feeling almost human again, he didn't bother with any clothing. He wanted two things. His bed and Claire.

"Take these."

Claire held out two tablets then a glass of water.

"Drink it all," she urged. "Stress can accelerate dehydration."

"I love that you know that." Finishing the last drop, Logan set the glass on the end table.

"My brain is my best asset," she said, leaning over to pick up the jeans Logan discarded on his way to the bathroom.

Admiring her firm, rounded backside, Logan grinned.

"Your brain. Your ass. Right now, it's a toss-up."

Claire smiled back. "I'm going to let that go because you've been such a good patient. Hardly a complaint to be heard."

"Hey," Logan called out when Claire headed for the door. "Where are you going?"

"You've had your shower. I need mine." Claire sighed. "I wish you would agree to stay at the main house for a few nights. I know the doctor cleared you. Still…"

"I hoped you would stay with me." *For once*, Logan added silently.

For a moment, he thought Claire was going to say no. He was ready with half a dozen arguments when she nodded.

"That will work." Claire pulled her shirt over her head. She removed her bra when she threw cold water on his dirty thoughts. "But no hanky-panky."

Before Logan could pull his chin off the floor, Claire closed the bathroom door. No sex? Come on. Hadn't he been good? He deserved a treat after the night he'd been through.

A few minutes later, Claire emerged with nothing but a skimpy towel covering her luscious body. Now that wasn't fair. How much was a man supposed to take?

Claire released her hair from the messy knot on top of her head. The long, blond tresses fell over her shoulders. Logan wondered if she did it deliberately. Tell him he wasn't getting any, then tease him with what he couldn't have. With one look at her face, Logan knew the answer. Claire was being Claire. It wasn't her fault that the mere thought of her made him ache.

"I'm going to borrow one of your t-shirts to sleep in."

"Why? I like you naked."

"I like you naked too," Claire said. "At this point, it's better to keep at least a thin layer of cotton between us."

"Do you honestly think that would stop me?"

Claire shook her head. She returned the shirt, dropped the towel, and climbed in beside him.

"I mean it, Logan. You need rest. Nothing more."

"If you let me hold you, I'll promise you anything."

"You might want to rethink that," Claire laughed, settling into his arms. "I might ask for something you aren't willing to part with."

"I can't imagine what that would be." Logan sighed with contentment. *I have everything I need right here.*

"Your truck?"

Logan felt the curve of Claire's lips against his chest. *Now* he had everything he needed. The only thing better than Claire was smiling Claire.

"My truck?" Logan pretended to consider the cost. "I could

probably get a couple hundred bucks for it on the open market. But having you spend the night? That is priceless."

The events of the evening finally caught up with them. The conversation faded away as they drifted off to sleep, locked in each other's arms.

Logan's last thoughts were ironic. It took almost getting his knee crushed by a baseball bat for Claire to finally agree to stay the night in his bed. Rafer was in jail. His knee was no worse for wear. His head hurt, but not excessively so. And Claire was soft and warm in his arms. All in all, the perfect ending to a very strange day.

That night changed their sleeping arrangements for good.

Without any fanfare, Claire moved a few of her things from the guest room in the main house to Logan's room above the garage. It was a small space. Keeping the bulk of her possessions where they were made sense. However, every night? She stayed with Logan. They made love. They talked for hours. Every morning, she woke up in his arms.

After a week, Logan was almost ready to send Rafer a thank you note. *Almost.* The knock on the head hadn't turned him into a raving lunatic.

Going to the police station to give their statements had been routine. No one questioned Logan and Claire's version of the events. Especially since Rafer's cohorts lost their nerve once they were sober enough to understand how much trouble they were in. They were happy to point fingers in any direction that took the heat off them.

As for Rafer's father-in-law, Rhonda called that one right. He didn't lift a finger to help. He refused his daughter's plea to post bail. Let the bastard rot was the general consensus.

That was when Rafer played his trump card. Or so he thought. Implicating Linda Sue Hemmings as the mastermind behind his attack on Logan gave Denville plenty of gossip to chew on. However, it didn't help Rafer get out of prison.

When the police went to question Linda Sue, they found out that she and her husband had left town early that morning. Linda Sue to a spa in New Mexico. Darryl on a business trip. Their sudden departure added gasoline to the already raging fires of speculation.

Was Rafer telling the truth? Was Linda Sue behind the attack on Logan? And what did Darryl know about his wife and her possibly illegal activities? Whatever the answers, it was certainly the juiciest thing to happen in these parts for as long as anyone could remember.

There was another bit of gossip that got as much play as Rafer and

Linda Sue. After the night that Logan was attacked, there was no way to keep it under wraps any longer. The whole town wanted to know. Was it true? Was Logan trying to resurrect his football career?

"Word was bound to get around." Jonas handed Logan a box of vodka. "Rafer shouted it so loudly I'm surprised they didn't hear it three states over. There were too many people around to keep it a secret."

"I know." Logan sighed. "I was hoping to get my team physical before the news broke. Answering questions from the media is a piece of cake compared to what I get here in Denville.

"Oh, get over yourself. No one cares about you." Rhonda winked at Jonas. She sat at the bar sipping her usual before-work Diet Coke. "We want to know how Claire acquired those mad skills with a gun."

"I've been curious about that myself," Jonas said. "With everything that's been going on, I haven't had a chance to ask."

All eyes turned to Claire, who was filling the top shelf behind the bar with newly washed glasses. Suddenly the center of attention, she paused, and then continued with her task.

"Logan knows." Claire shrugged. "It's no big deal."

"Are you kidding?" Rhonda exclaimed. "Not only was it dark, but the adrenaline had to be pumping through you like crazy. How did you hit Rafer's arm from that distance?"

"Luck?"

"Luck would have had you blowing the asshole's head off."

"Jesus, Rhonda," Claire chuckled, shaking her head. "That's a bit extreme."

"Rafer Macafee is a blight on this town. Always has been. Do you know he'll probably get away with only a slap on the wrist? Pug says Wade Eason will do more time than Rafer."

"Wade was the one who actually hit Logan over the head."

Jonas kept his head down, pretending to count bottles. It would be a long time before his stomach didn't do a sick flip when he thought about how close he came to losing Logan. An inch one way or the other and that two-by-four could have killed him.

Understanding, Claire reached over to squeeze Jonas' hand.

"For all his effort, Rafer didn't do any physical damage. Except to the recycling bin."

"Very funny, Logan." Rhonda absently stirred her Coke with her straw. "Aren't you pissed knowing Rafer will probably be free by the end of the week?"

"I'm not thrilled," Logan admitted. "On the other hand, I'm not going to waste my time thinking about Rafer."

"Nor should you," Jonas agreed. "Think of it this way, Rhonda. Everyone in Denville knows what Rafer did. His few friends either are in jail or have turned their backs on him. He has no blood relatives. His family by marriage has washed their hands of him."

"Even Cheryl?" Logan asked. Rafer's wife had put up with his drinking, his cheating – his general bad behavior. It was interesting to find out that *this* would be the final straw.

"Word has it she's filed for divorce. I guess her father gave her an ultimatum. Her husband or *his* money."

"Hallelujah to the power of the all mighty buck." Rhonda clapped her hands together. "Cheryl used to be a friend. When she took up with Rafer, she changed. Maybe with time, we can reconnect."

"Rafer is finished in Denville."

"Do you think he's smart enough to realize that?"

Jonas shrugged. "Who knows, Claire. He might gut it out for a while. He has no job. No place to live. I can't imagine he has much in the way of savings. If he has half a brain, he'll cut his losses. Move on to a new town where he can alienate a new community."

"Fingers crossed." Rhonda zeroed in on Claire. "So?"

"So?" Claire frowned. "What?"

"My gun. Your hand. Where did you learn to shoot like that?"

"God, you're like a dog with a bone."

"When it's this juicy? Damn straight."

"You might as well tell her, Claire," Logan said.

"Fine," Claire sighed.

"Goody." Rhonda patted the nearby stool. "Sit. Spill."

"I'll pour the coffee." Jonas reached for two cups.

"Don't get so excited." Claire joined Rhonda on the other side of the bar. "On the entertainment scale, the story barely rates a four."

"Logan?" Rhonda inquired, brows raised.

"I'd give it a solid eight." When he saw Claire's narrowed eyes, he smiled. "Sorry. You were under-selling it."

"And you're giving it too much build-up."

"Just tell us!"

"I was sixteen and there was a boy."

"At that age, there usually is," Rhonda nodded.

"I suppose," Claire acknowledged. "Brand Wycoff was my first real crush. He was tall and skinny with curly red hair."

"Was he older?"

"Naturally. A whole two years."

Claire and Rhonda shared a knowing look. When you were sixteen, eighteen seemed worldly by comparison. Especially when you compared sixteen-year-old boys.

"I wasn't ready to throw away my dreams for Brand. But I was ready to toss him my—"

Claire suddenly realized to whom she was talking. Sharing her youthful follies with Logan and Rhonda was one thing. Telling Jonas was another.

"You wanted to have sex with this boy," Jonas said matter-of-factly.

"Am I blushing?" Claire asked Logan.

After a close inspection of her face that ended in a quick kiss on the nose, Logan shook his head.

"Nope. Not a pink cheek in sight."

"It would be so much easier if I were a shrinking violet. A case of the vapors and I could gracefully ease out of this conversation."

"Do women still get the vapors?" Jonas speculated.

"Who cares," Rhonda growled in frustration. "Finish the story. You were about to get down and dirty with Ginger Boy?"

"Right." Claire laughed.

She was surrounded by friends. If you couldn't share your most embarrassing moments with them, what was the point?

"After extensive research, I discovered Brand loved guns. That right there should have given me pause. But I plead the idiocy of youth. Plus, like in Denville, where I grew up, almost everybody owned some kind of firearm."

"You learned everything you could about guns?" Rhonda asked, impressed by Claire's dedication. When she was that age, had she simply batted her eyes? Then again, all that had gotten her was Elmer and years of heartache. Claire's way seemed much smarter.

"Way more than necessary, as it turned out." Claire smiled her thanks when Jonas filled up her coffee cup. "After a few months of hanging out with friends, Brand finally asked if I wanted to shoot some tin cans out back of his folks' place."

"Smooth." Logan rolled his eyes.

Claire stuck out her tongue. "It worked. Of course, at that point, almost anything would have. I was the proverbial ripe plum."

"Don't let Logan give you any guff," Rhonda laughed. "I knew him when he was eighteen. He picked plums right and left."

"Thanks for that, Rhonda." Logan playfully jabbed a knuckle into her side, causing Rhonda to laugh even harder.

"My story is coming to its rather non-climactic ending. Are you still interested?"

"Sorry." Rhonda sobered, her eyes twinkling. "You say non-climactic. Does that mean you and Red didn't have sex? Or was it really bad?"

"I made the mistake of being a better shot than he was." Claire could still see the look of disbelief on Brand's face when she hit five of the six cans. "My first lesson. I swear it was the first time I had ever shot a gun. Brand didn't believe me."

"Naturally," Rhonda scoffed.

"Suffice it to say, Brand was not my first lover. I did like shooting, though. I still hit the gun range now and then."

"Who was your first?"

"Rhonda!"

"What?"

"You wanted to know why I was a good shot and I told you."

"Oh, come on, Claire." Rhonda leaned a little closer. "We've opened the can of worms. Let them breathe."

"Do worms breathe?" Claire shook the question off. "I'm not getting into a debate about worms."

"Thank God."

"Exactly," Claire nodded at Jonas. "Three more words about the start of my sex life. College. Sophomore year."

"But—"

"That's it, Rhonda." Claire laughed. She gathered up her cup, reaching over the bar to put it in the sink. "The rest is classified under nobody's business but my own."

Hours later, lying in each other's arms after making love, Logan smoothed back Claire's thick, glossy hair.

"Why didn't you tell Dad and Rhonda the whole story?"

Claire tucked Logan's arm tighter around her waist. Sex with him was the best she had ever known. Better than any fantasy. The cuddling after ran a close second to her favorite part.

They had a connection. Before. During. After. It made telling him her deepest, darkest secrets easier.

"The mood was light." Claire sighed. "They didn't need to know that Brand Wycoff turned out to be a bastard."

"He hit you."

"Yes."

Brand didn't take a woman besting him with good grace. Instead, he backhanded Claire so hard her lip was swollen for two days.

"My only regret is that I didn't kick his balls up into his throat."

"You did the smart thing, Claire. You left and didn't go back."

"I left Brand free to abuse another woman. We both know I wasn't the first. Or the last."

"You were sixteen. What were your options?"

In a small town where Brand's daddy ran things? Claire options had been nonexistent. She went home. Put ice on her lip. And kept her mouth shut. It wasn't brave. However, as Logan said, it was smart.

One good thing came from her brief relationship. More than ever, Claire was determined to make her own way in the world. Far away from Iowa.

"What's so funny?" Logan tipped Claire's chin up, happy to see her smile.

"My life. I swore the closest I would ever get to a small town again would be a flyover in a very large airplane. Not only am I living in Denville? The town I left is only five hundred miles north of here."

"We could be there by lunch."

Claire shuddered. "Bite your tongue."

"Thank you."

"You're welcome." Claire's kiss was lingering and sweet. "Now tell me what I did."

"You trusted me with the Bastard Brand story. Had you told anyone before?"

"You were the first." Because she *did* trust him. Because she knew with every fiber of her being that Logan was the only person she would ever feel comfortable with to share... everything.

"Thank you."

Logan turned off the bedside lamp then pulled Claire close. She listened as his breathing became even and sleep overtook him. She was tired. So much had happened in such a short period.

Claire's thoughts drifted. The past few months had been the happiest of her life. Every minute filled with work and Logan. From the very beginning, they had a goal. It united them in a way few people would ever understand. The night they met, they felt an instant connection that grew stronger every day. For all of this to work, it had to.

The trust Logan mentioned went both ways. If they didn't believe in each other, they would have failed before they began.

Soon, they would take the next step. Not a leap of faith like back in December when Logan put his future in her hands. When they left Denville for Seattle, their paths would diverge. Claire wondered if Logan realized that yet. To finish the journey, they had to do it separately. That was the only way they could both succeed.

She let herself relax into much-needed slumber. May and then June. That was all the time they had left before everything changed. She vowed to make the most of it.

Claire knew what tomorrow would bring. It was still her job to prepare Logan the best way she knew how. After that? The Seattle Knights. That was the unknown. For both of them.

IT WAS THE hottest June that anyone in Denville could remember. The green of a rainy spring would soon fade to a brittle brown if the record heat continued.

"I'll bet you're glad you're getting out of here." Rhonda handed Claire a pair of jeans. "Seattle is rainy, right?"

"It can be." Claire tucked her makeup bag into the corner of her suitcase. "It's a myth that there is nothing but day after day of gray skies and drizzle."

Rhonda sat on the bed with a sigh. She was dressed for the heat. Blue tank top and matching shorts were not only weather-appropriate, but they also did wonders for her curvy figure.

"I can't believe you're leaving. Denville will revert to Dullsville without you and Logan."

Claire did one last tour of the room, checking drawers for any stray items. It wouldn't be a disaster if she left something behind. If it were important, Jonas could send it to her. However, she wouldn't use a stray article of clothing as an excuse to stay in touch. When she called Logan's father, it would be because she wanted nothing more than to talk.

The same went for Rhonda. Their friendship was not something Claire would let slide – no matter how many miles separated them. Besides, she had a wedding to come back for. Which reminded her.

"About your wedding."

"No." Rhonda shook her head. Her ponytail made a vigorous flip. "You can't bail on your maid-of-honor commitment."

"I wasn't planning to. I did want you to know that I might not be able to take part in any pre-wedding festivities. October is right in the middle of football season. I'll be here for the ceremony, but that will probably be it."

Claire zipped up her bag. She came with one and she was leaving with one. Everything in the training room was staying. The oils, lotions, balms. She wanted them to be here whenever Logan visited his father. She didn't think about coming back with him. That was still part of the great unknown.

"Don't worry about that," Rhonda said with a wave of her red-tipped fingers. "We've moved the wedding to March."

"What?" Claire set the suitcase by the door before turning. "Why?"

"Pug and I want you *and* Logan at our wedding. We think of you as our good luck charms. By March, all the Super Bowl hoopla should be over. Logan will be free to join all the festivities."

"Please tell me you haven't mentioned any of this to Logan." Claire felt her stomach clench. "He's already under so much pressure. Especially now that the national media picked up the story."

A throwaway online post about a fight in the parking lot of a bar in Oklahoma was somehow seen by a blogger. The blogger was seen by a local stringer for ESPN. It started slowly. A phone call asking for a quote. The request for an interview. Before long, someone was bound to show up in Denville with a camera.

Logan's story was gaining traction.

"I swear." Rhonda held up her hand. "Logan won't know anything about our change of plans. We want him to succeed, Claire. We want the same for you."

"Thanks, Rhonda. I want that too."

Which was why Claire was getting out of Denville.

"What I don't understand is why you're leaving today. Why not wait and go with Logan at the end of the week?"

"I'd like to know the answer to that myself."

Crap. It served her right. Her plan had always been to speak with Logan before she left. Why wasn't he at the bar instead of overhearing her conversation with Rhonda?

"Logan…"

"That's my cue." Rhonda hopped off the bed. She threw her arms around Claire. "Everyone will be mad as all get out if you don't stop by *Lefty's* on your way out of town."

Claire hugged Rhonda, her eyes locked with Logan's. Usually, she had no problem reading what he was thinking. For the first time, his eyes were void of emotion.

"Don't worry. I won't forget."

"Logan." Rhonda stopped in front of her old friend. Her eyes darted back and forth between him and Claire, a worried frown wrinkling her brow.

"Go." Logan patted her arm reassuringly. "It will be okay."

"I wasn't going to sneak away," Claire said when they were alone.

"Really?" Logan wandered through the room, checking the dresser drawers, then the closet. "Looks to me like I was last on your list before you hit the road. Forgetting that last thing can be easy."

Claire hated to hear the hurt in his voice. When his eyes met hers again, the hard steel in them made her flinch. She had seen Logan's anger. She had never felt it turned on her.

"Sit." Claire sank onto the bed, patting the mattress. "Please."

Reluctantly, Logan joined her. Not nearby as she asked. On the other side. Out of touching range. With a resigned sigh, Claire gathered her thoughts. This was important. She needed Logan to understand. That meant being *clear* and *unemotional*. The way she felt, she would be lucky if she managed *clear*.

"I'm not leaving you."

Without a word, Logan's shifted his gaze to her suitcase. When he looked back, his eyes said in big, bold letters — **BULLSHIT***!*

"Listen to my words. Yes. I'm leaving Denville. *I am not leaving you.*" Claire swallowed. "Unless you want me to."

"Oh, no." Logan shot to his feet and began pacing. "You don't get to turn this on me. You're the one with one foot out the door. *Without* telling me you were going."

"I know. I—"

Logan cut her off. "When I left you in bed this morning, warm and soft from our lovemaking, you didn't say a word that it was the last time. You smiled when I kissed you goodbye." Logan clapped both hands on his head, his fingers pulling at his hair. "That was your goodbye, wasn't it? A final fuck. I guess I should be grateful you were giving me that much. Except you liked it, didn't you? There was no faking that. Why not get off one more time?"

"Don't be mean, Logan." Claire reminded herself he was hurt. However, that didn't mean she had to sit and take his insults. "Don't say something you're going to regret."

"At the moment, I can't think of what that would be."

"Trust me, you're damn close. Please. Listen. Don't say anything until I finish."

"Why?"

"Because deep down you know I wouldn't be leaving unless I had a good reason."

Claire waited. It took him a while but eventually Logan's shoulders began to relax. Slowly, he walked back to the bed. This time, when he sat, it was next to her.

"Thank you."

"Tell me, Claire."

There he was. In Logan's eyes, she saw the man she knew. Wary, yes. But the anger was tempered. He was ready to listen.

"We've been isolated, Logan." Claire chose her words carefully. "I had a plan when I came here. It was simple. Get us both to the NFL."

"Has that changed?"

"The plan? No. But we weren't supposed to become personally involved. That's on me."

"Do you regret that we're lovers?"

"I wouldn't change anything." Claire gently cupped Logan's cheek. "Not a second."

"So…?"

"You can take me to Seattle as your girlfriend. No one would bat an eye." Claire sighed. "If I'm going to be taken seriously, *I can't go as your girlfriend*. Do you understand?"

Unfortunately, Logan did. As a woman, she already had a big strike against her in a male-dominated business. Claire would be held to a higher standard. Her every move scrutinized. A *man* trying to make the team could sleep with anyone he wanted. A *woman* sleeping with that *man*? She would be committing professional suicide.

"Fucking double-standard."

Claire smiled with relief. Leave it to Logan to boil it down to the bare basics.

"You're garnering some national attention. It's only a matter of time before an enterprising reporter comes sniffing around Denville. I can't be here when that happens."

"And we can't leave together." Logan nodded. "I get it, Claire."

"Gaige is sending a car for me. It should be here in a few hours." Seeing Logan's look, Claire shook her head. "He doesn't know about us."

"He isn't a fool. One look and he'll know something is going on."

"We'll deal with that when it happens." Claire waited. When Logan opened his arms, she sank in with a grateful sigh. "The plan always was for you to stay with Gaige. His house is so big you could go weeks without seeing each other if you wanted. I'll move back into my apartment."

"One more thing." Logan pulled back enough to look Claire straight in the eye. "Are you using this as an excuse to dump me?"

"What? Have you been listening to anything I've said?"

"I need to hear it, Claire." Logan steadied his gaze. It was clear and direct. It looked right into Claire's soul.

"I'm not walking out of your life. You're stuck with me, Logan."

"That's all I needed to hear."

Logan grabbed the front of Claire's t-shirt, ripping it in half.

"We've never played 'You, Tarzan. Me, Jane.'" Claire's eyes twinkled. If Logan wanted to be King of the Jungle, she was fine with that.

Logan pushed her back onto the bed, his mouth claiming hers in a deep, commanding kiss. His teeth nipped the side of her neck, and then he whispered words that made her shiver from head to toe.

"I'm not playing, Claire. Get ready for the ride of your life."

CHAPTER FIFTEEN

CLAIRE LIKED TO be in control.

From the time she was a small girl, to get what she wanted, she knew she had to be the one to call the shots. She left her hometown on her own terms. Worked hard. Even when Gaige Benson offered her a hand up, Claire made sure she knew the terms before she agreed.

It was the same with her lovers. Claire was the aggressor. She never invited a man into her bed with a long-term commitment in mind. She liked sex. When she felt an itch, she found the right man to help her scratch it – then she moved on.

Logan wasn't like the men in her past. He didn't wait for her to make the first move. He didn't expect her to guide his moves. He took as much as he gave. To Claire's surprise and delight, the result was the best sex of her life.

Logan fit her perfectly. One of the things she liked best was his unpredictability. Sex could be lighthearted. It could be intense. Claire never knew what mood they would be in.

However, this was the first time Logan had come to her full-on Alpha. He trapped her arms above her head. He controlled the action. Claire knew she could never live on a constant diet of being ordered around – but today? At this moment? She loved every second.

"You belong to me."

Logan breathed the words over her skin. It felt like they entered her body. Into her bloodstream. Into her soul.

Claire arched her neck, begging Logan to kiss. Bite. Devour. The air rushed from her lungs when he complied.

"Say it, Claire. Tell me you're mine."

She was. Claire knew she would never feel like this with any other man. It wasn't about giving Logan control. It was about letting go. Of the past. Of now. Of the future. For the first time in her life, she wanted to belong to someone. She wanted Logan to belong to her. It had to work both ways.

"Are you mine?"

Logan lifted his head. His eyes were a rich, chocolate brown. Molten. Claire could feel herself sinking. She felt a moment of panic. Giving up temporary control was one thing. This was another. She didn't want to drown. She didn't want to lose herself in a man – not even Logan.

Claire was about to pull away when Logan smiled. It was slightly wicked and all man. But it, and his words, told her what she needed to know.

"I was yours the moment I saw you."

"That night in the bar? You knew it then?"

"I knew I could trust you with my life." Logan's kiss was firm. Masterful. His tongue touched the tips of Claire's, pulling away when she tried to draw him in. Taking her torn shirt, Logan tied Claire's hands together.

"Are you mine?"

This time, when she heard the question, Claire didn't hesitate.

"Yes. Yours. Only yours, Logan."

Logan smiled with satisfaction.

"Grab the headboard." When she did, Logan nodded. "Good. Don't move. If those hands don't stay where they are, I'll make sure they do."

Claire licked her lips. Her instinct was to make a smart-ass remark. Not this time. It was Logan's show. All she wanted was to hop on for the sexy ride.

"You have the best bras." Logan flipped open the front clasp, laying her breasts open to his gaze. "Were you thinking of me when you put it on this morning?"

"I'm always thinking of you." It was damn near the truth.

"I like that." Logan sucked one nipple into his mouth – hard and fast. Claire's back arched off the bed. "Let me give you a whole lot more to think about."

Logan took his time. He kissed. He caressed. He teased. By the time he reached the waistband of her jeans, Claire panted as though she had run a marathon. She wanted everything he was giving her. And more. So much more.

"Are you ready for me, Claire?" Logan slid the denim down her legs, blindly tossing them across the room.

"You know I am."

Claire couldn't keep her hips still. She would have wrapped her legs around Logan, drawing him close, if he hadn't given her a warning look. He set the pace, not her. With difficulty, she kept as still as possible.

"Mmm. Very nice. Lace." Logan ran one finger along the edge of her panties. "You're going to need new ones."

The sound of lace tearing only managed to ramp up Claire's desire. The cool air against her heated center was brief. To her delight, Logan's hot mouth didn't give her time to cool down.

"So sweet," he whispered. His tongue took another taste. "Honey with a touch of spice."

Claire gripped the headboard, letting Logan take her on a rollercoaster ride. Up, up, up. Then, just as she thought she reached the peak, he eased her down, the dip frustrating, yet still exciting.

This went on for what seemed like a blessed eternity. Claire called Logan's name. Pleaded for release. His response was to take her even higher. His mouth. His hands. He played her like the maestro he was. Her body was his willing instrument.

"Now. Come for me, Claire."

Wave after wave. The feelings never seemed to end. Lights burst behind her closed eyelids. Red. Yellow. Blue. Not a rainbow. A kaleidoscope. The patterns changed in a constant wave. Unique. Breathtakingly beautiful.

She didn't know how it was possible. She felt spent. Yet the second Logan covered her body with his. The instant he entered her, it started again. The climb. The reaching. Only this time, it was better because he was with her every step of the way. They rode, side by side, to the top. The crash over was all the sweeter because this time, Logan shouted her name the same instant she shouted his.

This was how it was supposed to be, Claire thought as one more wave of pleasure crashed over her. Not nice. Not an easy slide toward a tension-easing orgasm. Her heart almost pounded out of her chest. Every inch of her skin tingled with a million sparks of pleasure. She couldn't do this to herself. No one else knew how to make her toes curl.

It was Logan. Only Logan. Forever Logan.

CHAPTER SIXTEEN

SEATTLE HAD NEVER been home.

Logan watched as the city rolled by from his vantage point in the front seat of Gaige's silver Jaguar. He had planned to make the city his home. The feel of it appealed to him. Then and now.

When he was a rookie, he saw Seattle as a young city. Plenty to do and see. People his own age from varying and interesting walks of life. Logan had anticipated a long, happy relationship. With the city. And with the Knights.

Neither happened.

This time, Logan saw things from a different perspective. A little older. Hopefully wiser. He wasn't worried about what the city had to offer him. He thought about what he could offer the city.

"If I make the team, I want to give back to the community."

"I like the sound of that," Gaige said. He turned off the highway toward his home on Lake Washington. "Except for one thing."

"What's that?"

"Cut the '*if* I make the team' crap. Claire says you're ready. Maybe better than your first go-round."

Claire.

It had been a week since she left Denville. They spoke every day. Skype made it easy to *see* her whenever he wanted. Touching her was another matter. Logan felt better knowing they were in the same city.

"She's been keeping the team and me up-to-date on your progress. Harry is excited to see you in action."

Harry Coleman, the Knights head coach had always been one of

Logan's biggest supporters. It was good to know that hadn't changed.

"I still need to pass the physical."

"Claire doesn't seem to think that will be a problem." Gaige glanced at Logan. "Any reason you're worried?"

"General nerves, that's all."

"Nothing wrong with that. Learn how to manage them and nerves can be a powerful asset." Gaige gave a laugh. "Trust me, I know."

"After all this time? Really?"

"You get nervous when something matters. I'm still playing because I love the game, Logan. It means something."

Logan frowned. "Then why quit? Why walk away when you still love what you're doing?"

Gaige turned into the driveway of the home he had spent the last five years building to his exact specifications.

Classic. Modern. Gaige hadn't worried about pigeonholing the style. The lines were bold and sweeping. Three stories. He wanted what he wanted. As with all things in life, that was what he got.

"Impressive."

Logan carried his bags through the four-car garage and into the house. He took in the high ceilings, the open space. He didn't know much about interior decorating. The colors were mellow with pops of color provided by paintings Logan imagined were worth a mid-sized fortune.

When Logan first met Gaige, the QB was already a superstar. His tastes reflected a lifestyle that was a far cry from his humble beginnings. Gaige was polished. Sophisticated. However, he never completely let go of the dirty street-fighter roots. He knew how to pick the perfect wine. However, that didn't mean he couldn't beat the shit out of someone in a bar fight.

Gaige lived in a house worth millions. He came from nothing. He had managed to blend the two. Embrace the new. Never forget the old.

"Come on. I'll show you to your room, and then we can grab a couple of beers on the deck." Gaige slapped Logan on the back as they ascended the long, curving staircase.

"The second floor is my playground." Gaige didn't pause, heading directly for another set of stairs. "Feel free to come down here anytime you like. The workout room is to your left, the other way leads to the game room."

Logan looked down the hall with interest.

"What kind of games?"

"Most of my misspent youth consisted of stealing smokes from my mother's purse and video games. Luckily, I lost my taste for cigarettes." At the top of the stairs, Gaige turned left. "You'll find the usual suspects in the way of games. My gang and I ruled the neighborhood arcade. God, I was such a stereotype. Looking back, I wasn't as tough as I thought."

But tougher than any kid should have to be, Gaige added mentally.

"I want you to make yourself at home. My room is on the other side of the house, so you have complete privacy." Gaige opened a door at the end of the hall. "I think you'll like the view."

After seeing the rest of Gaige's house, Logan expected the wall of windows that showcased Lake Washington. What surprised him was the best view of all. Standing in the middle of the room was Claire.

"Welcome to Seattle."

"Dinner will be ready in two hours," Gaige said. Then he laughed. "If you need more time to catch up, let me know."

Before the door closed, Claire was in Logan's arms.

They kissed as if they had been apart for years, falling onto the bed. Clothing was pushed aside instead of removed. They came together in a heated rush that left them breathless and satisfied.

"That was…"

"Thrilling? Exciting? Mind-blowingly intense?" Claire asked. She was sprawled on top of Logan, happy to stay that way.

"I was going to say unexpected." Logan chuckled. "But I like your words better."

He couldn't stop touching her. The desperation was gone, but the need to stay connected was constant. Logan laced his fingers with hers and felt himself settle for the first time since she left him in Denville.

"Not that I'm complaining," Logan said after a few minutes of easy silence. "I thought we were keeping this on the down-low."

"Blame Gaige." Claire kissed Logan's exposed stomach. "I met him here for lunch the day after I got back. Partly to catch up and partly for a face-to-face on your status. I hadn't been here five minutes before he figured out that we had developed a *very* personal relationship."

"I guess he's fine with that?"

"Now," Claire nodded. "First, he reamed me out. *You're trying to build a reputation as a professional*, he said in that quiet quarterback voice of his."

"Oh, I remember that voice."

"It's unforgettable. You feel like you've let him down."

"And no one wants to let *Gaige* down."

"Turns out he had suspected something was going on for months. Apparently, I'm even worse at hiding things over the phone than I am in person."

"What now?"

Claire slid to Logan's side, letting her leg wrap around his. Facing him, she smoothed a hand over his face. She sighed. *What a face it was.* She had to remember to ask Gaige what his first thoughts had been when he saw the short-haired, clean-shaven Logan. Such a difference from when they met last December.

"Nothing has changed." She smiled when he raised an eyebrow. "Outside of Gaige knowing about us. The plan is the same. I'll still be around to workout with you. But from here on? It's going to be you and Gaige. He knows the Knights better than anyone. He'll be your secret weapon, Logan. When training camp starts, you'll be ready."

Logan closed his eyes when Claire rested her head on his chest. Did she realize her hand was over his heart? Did she know that it was hers?

Now wasn't the time to tell her. Not when there were still so many questions for which he didn't have the answers.

Would he make the team? Would his knee hold up? Was his future here or back in Denville?

Only when he knew the answers to those questions could he ask Claire to share her life with him. She needed to know what she was getting into. Running back or bartender? He didn't think she would care which it was. He was the one who had to know. One way or the other.

"DAMN, KID. I don't remember those moves. Let me see that again. And Sol? Don't hold back. We're going at full speed."

Gaige's backyard had become their football field. For over a month, they had gone through the same drills they would face when training camp opened in less than three weeks.

It was becoming harder and harder to tamp down his excitement.

The first major hurdle was behind him. The team physical. No one was giving Logan a pass because of his history with the organization. Logan didn't want them to. There was too much at stake for everyone involved.

Logan knew what to expect. He went through the same thing out of college before he signed his first professional contract. The big difference was that this time they paid particular attention to his surgically repaired knee.

After the routine examination, a new set of x-rays was taken followed by an MRI. The team doctor and trainer wanted time to look them over and consult. If they were happy with what they saw, Logan would be taken through endurance drills. Included? The stress tests on his knee.

Proof once more that Claire was a genius. Her program not only strengthened his knee. It also prepared him mentally. The adrenaline pumping through him had been more anticipation than anxiety.

Because of Claire, he knew he was ready. Because of her, he passed every potential obstacle with flying colors.

Gaige handed off the ball to Logan. Sol Fellows, the big Knights linebacker, was deceptively fast. His bread and butter was feasting on cocky running backs who thought they could sprint past his imposing bulk.

A few years ago, Logan was one of those idiots. Now, he appreciated what men like Sol brought to the game. Experience. Instinct. Before he stepped on the field, Sol knew his opponents. He studied their moves. He prepared – mentally *and* physically.

Logan knew what he was up against. Sol was in his prime. One of the best in the game. Logan took the ball from Gaige. Using his repaired knee, he faked right, then left. Then, he blew past Sol like he was standing still.

Amazed, Sol looked at his empty arms. It should have been full of gimpy running back. Then he looked at Logan and grinned.

"Damn, Gaige. We got ourselves a runner."

Watching as Logan did a victory lap, Gaige nodded. "He's better than he used to be."

"That's because he's added brains to his repertoire. He was always fast. His instincts were good."

"Maturity. It hits us all eventually. Some guys don't find it until after they've hung up their cleats."

"True." Sol took the bottle of water Gaige offered. "With the kid, we could be good for another five or six years."

"I know what you're saying, Sol. I won't change my mind about retiring."

Gaige picked up a towel to wipe the sweat from his face. The early summer day was pleasantly warm if you were out for a casual stroll.

What they were doing in his backyard wasn't casual. This was going to be his last season. Not matter what. After all these years, he refused to go out anything but a winner.

"You'll miss it."

"I'd say it's only a game, Sol. But we both know that's bullshit."

"The game is everything." Sol said the words with the reverence they deserved.

"Damn right." Gaige tapped his bottle against Sol's.

It was time to find something else. Gaige knew his body could survive a few more seasons. His mind needed a new path to pursue. He still loved football. His greatest fear was losing that love. He was close to burning out. Devoting his life to something, day in and day out, for close to thirty years, there had to come a time when he was ready to walk away. For Gaige Benson, that time was fast approaching.

"What the hell will you do with yourself? The idea of retirement scares the hell out of me." Sol shuddered at the thought.

"I have no idea what I'm going to do." Gaige's famous smile widened. "But I'm looking forward to finding out."

CHAPTER SEVENTEEN

LOGAN FELT LIKE a child on his first day of school.
The Seattle Knights training camp opened with the usual buzz from the media and fans. Who will make the team? Who will surprise the experts as a breakout player? Who will be a bust? Will this be *our* year?

Logan was enough of a story to garner a bit of attention. It wasn't a distraction for him or the team. The players he knew from before welcomed him back. The men fighting for a spot on the roster were another matter. Logan was competition. Older. He had been here before.

None of the rookies was overtly hostile. More like wary. Friendships off the field were one thing. Once you stepped between the hash marks, it was every man for himself.

Logan might be apprehensive. *Claire* was close to throwing up.

If she didn't care so much, she could stand on the sidelines – professional. Detached. It would be easier. However, it wouldn't be half as much fun. She had a horse in this race. A big, sleek, beautiful stud. She couldn't cheer aloud. However, inside she was screaming like a madwoman.

Logan only looked her way one time. Right before he took the field. Something passed between them, as it always did when their eyes met. It calmed them both.

Claire's stomach settled.

Logan showed the coaching staff, the media, and the fans that he was back. After the first week, there was little doubt that he was in shape and determined to make the team. It was early, but some were already predicting he wouldn't just be on the roster. If his knee held up, Logan Price would start on opening day.

"I'VE MISSED YOU."

Claire smiled. There was nothing better than naked Logan. Unless it was her on top of him. After they had made love. Or during. Or before. Honestly? She would take Logan any way she could get him.

"It's been four days."

"An eternity," Logan proclaimed.

She couldn't argue. Yesterday, the Knights had played their third, and most important, preseason game. The starters stayed in for most of the first half. The players fighting for their football lives were given another chance to impress.

Instead of flattening out as most people expected, Logan's performance continued to wow both his critics and supporters. Gaige kept telling him that he was on the team. It was a done deal. However, until the official word came down, he wasn't counting his chickens.

"I can't believe Harry Coleman didn't tell you after the game. How much more are you expected to do?"

Claire felt Logan's frustration – and he felt hers. The assistant trainer's job was still out there. She felt like it was being dangled like a juicy carrot. Tantalizingly close. As soon as she thought she had it, they jerked it away. Not out of sight. Just a few inches. Enough to keep her hopeful.

"The good news is coming," Logan assured her. "For both of us."

She hoped so. Claire was ready for a change. Her job as a masseuse at a day spa in Renton wasn't terribly fulfilling. Her clients were mostly rich women with a few hours to kill in the middle of the day. If she had to hear one more pampered trophy wife complain about how hard it was to find decent caviar, Claire thought her head would explode.

However, it paid the bills while she waited for the Knights to get off their asses and give her the job of her dreams.

"I need food."

Claire scrambled out of bed before jogging to the bathroom. As always, Logan enjoyed the view, brief as it was. He would have liked a slow saunter, but not from the woman he knew. She never walked when she could run. She had things to do and no time to waste.

Luckily, the one time she slowed down was in bed. Logan could spend hours exploring her beautiful body. To his delight, Claire let him. Then she happily returned the favor.

"What are you hungry for?" he called out.

Claire stuck her head through the door. She was grinning. "What do you think?"

"Pizza."

What else? It was Claire's go-to food craving. Reaching for his phone, Logan called the nearby place that delivered. They usually stayed in. Gaige was a gracious host. Either they barbecued or Claire would cook something healthy. Indulging her occasional guilty pleasure was fine with him.

Well, he would have skipped the whole-wheat crust, added cheese and piled on the meat. He hated to break it to her, but sauce and vegetables on cardboard wasn't his idea of pizza. Or anyone else's.

As a reward for being so clever, Claire blew Logan a kiss before disappearing into the bathroom.

Logan placed the order, already planning to raid Gaige's well-stocked refrigerator after Claire left for the night. The ice cream was his favorite treat. She knew he cheated with the occasional bowl of Mocha Almond Fudge. The fact that she never called him out on it made him love her more.

He could hear the sound of running water and was about to join Claire for some steamy, wet fun when his phone signaled an incoming text.

Get your ass downstairs. Now. We have company.

Logan frowned at the screen. *Company?* That meant *don't bring Claire.* They had successfully hidden their relationship from everyone except for two close, trusted members of the Knights. One was Sol Fellows.

Sean McBride was the other. The wide receiver was a close friend then and now. Sean refused to let Logan drop him after he went back to Oklahoma. Once a week without fail, Sean emailed him. He called at least once a month.

At first, Logan didn't answer. Rather than give up, Sean showed up in Denville with no warning. They shared a beer, and then Sean turned around and flew home. Before he left, he warned Logan that if he were forced to make a return trip, he would kick his ass. Logan believed him. From then on, all emails and phone calls were promptly answered.

Logan dressed quickly. Instead of leaving Claire a note, he left his phone with the text on his pillow.

Laughter reached Logan before he was halfway down the staircase. It appeared Gaige and his guest were out on the deck. And in a good mood. That was a good sign. His curiosity growing, Logan walked through the open French doors.

"Logan," Gaige called out. "Grab a beer and join us."

Logan did as Gaige suggested but he didn't know how he would swallow the alcohol. Standing five feet away was the Seattle Knights head coach. Why would Harry Coleman be there unless it was bad news? If Logan had made the team, Harry could have told him anytime on the flight home from Denver.

This is it, Logan thought. *All the hard work. The raised expectations. His last chance. Over.* It looked like he was going back to Denville after all.

"Coach." Logan shook the other man's hand.

Harry Coleman was considered old school by most of the league. Sixty years old. He looked like every one of them. Rumpled was a kind way of describing his style. Jeans. T-shirt. A jacket with the Knights logo over his heart. Tall and thin, the man bled blue and gold.

Harry loved his wife, his kids, and his team.

All that mattered to his players was his knowledge of the game and his steadfast loyalty. If they played hard and kept their nose clean, Harry had their back.

Logan knew Harry lobbied hard for the Knights to give him another chance. It was good of the head coach to come here instead of cutting him in a more public way. It showed what a classy individual Harry Coleman was.

"Christ," Harry said in his unmistakable, booming voice. "The kid looks like he's going to his execution. I thought you wanted to play for the Knights."

"I do." Logan sighed. "More than anything. It's... Wait. What are you saying?"

He looked from Harry to Gaige. They were smiling. No. Grinning. One wasn't that happy when delivering bad news. Right?

"You made the team, kid." Harry's laugh rang out over the deck and probably across Lake Washington.

"You're sure?"

It wasn't the brightest of reactions, but Logan was stunned. To go from thinking the worst to finding out he'd made it, was disorienting. It took him a few seconds for it to sink in.

Logan Price was back. He was a member of the Seattle Knights football team.

"You're not going to faint, are you, kid?" Gaige's words teased, but just in case, he put a steadying hand on Logan's shoulder.

"I'm fine." Logan let out a whoop. "Holy shit, Gaige. Holy shit."

Grabbing Gaige, he gave him a bone-crushing hug. It was Gaige's belief in him that was the start of all this. He would never be able to repay him.

"Easy. The last thing I need is for my QB and starting running back to injure themselves before the season starts."

Harry shook his head as he watched them hop around. It was part of what made them fierce competitors. The boys inside the men. Yes, football was a multi-billion dollar business. However, the real secret to success was to never forget that, at its heart, it was just a game. Be serious when necessary, but play like a bunch of ten-year-olds.

Gaige hadn't lost sight of his inner child. It was good to see that neither had Logan.

Finding the lump in his throat had magically dissolved, Logan grabbed his beer and took a long pull. When Harry's words finally sunk in, he spit a mouthful across the deck, barely missing Gaige.

"Did you say *starting* running back?"

"Promise me you'll pay better attention during the games," Harry admonished, with a twinkle in his eyes. "You earned it, Logan. Congratulations."

Instead of jumping with excitement, this time, Logan collapsed onto a nearby chair. It was too much all at once. Making the team *and* starting? It would take a while before his legs could hold his weight.

Understanding, Gaige let him absorb the news.

"Can I get you another beer, Harry?"

"Nope. I need to get home." Harry slapped Logan on the back. "Enjoy the moment, kid. I'll give you until practice on Wednesday. Then I expect you to work as if you're still fighting for that job. Deal?"

"Deal." Tentatively, Logan pushed to his feet. Steady, he shook Harry's hand. "Thanks, coach."

"Win us some games. That will be thanks enough."

Harry was almost out the door when another thought hit Logan.

"What about Claire?" When he saw Harry's confused frown, Logan's heart sank. Harry never forgot a name. This couldn't be good.

"Claire Thornton," Gaige said pointedly. "The woman who rehabbed Logan's knee?"

"Right," Harry nodded. "You thought she would be a good assistant trainer."

"Cut the crap, Harry." Gaige had known his head coach too long not to recognize when the man knew something he wasn't sharing. "You know what the deal was. If Logan made the team, management would give Claire serious consideration for the job. I'd say she's more than proven her worth."

"She's a miracle worker, Harry." Logan wasn't going to let Claire's chance slip away. Harry had to understand that without her, Logan would still be walking around Denville in a haze of self-pity.

"Harry." Gaige waited until his head coach looked him straight in the eye. "What's going on?"

"Officially?"

"Shit," Gaige slammed his bottle onto the table. Foam shot out in an angry burst, perfectly mirroring his and Logan's feelings. "If there is an unofficial version, Claire is well and truly screwed over. Go ahead, Harry. Give us the company line."

"No one is disputing what your friend has accomplished. You say her program got Logan back on the field, I believe you. The worry upstairs is that you are *too* close to the situation. It's a relationship that could cause tension in the locker room."

Logan almost exploded. If he understood what Harry was saying, management thought Claire was using Gaige to sleep her way into a job. *Fuck.* She'd called it. A woman couldn't put a foot out of place. The fact that she wasn't involved with Gaige didn't matter. It was all about perception.

The only thing that kept Logan from jumping to Claire's defense was that Gaige beat him to it.

"We discussed this back when I brought the idea to you, Harry. I assured you there was nothing between Claire and me except friendship. Do you doubt my word?"

"No."

"Then what the hell is going on?" Logan could keep silent only so long. Claire had earned her chance. A chance, according to Gaige, management had agreed to give her.

"They wanted to keep their franchise quarterback happy. No one believed Logan would pass the physical, let alone make the team. What was the harm in letting you think your friend would seriously be considered for the job?" Harry knew it sounded bad. Because it was.

"Who exactly are *they*?"

Gaige asked exactly what Logan was wondering. They waited impatiently for Harry to answer.

"Gaige..."

"Now is the time for the unofficial explanation, Harry. Though it isn't hard to figure it out."

"What?" Logan demanded.

When Harry didn't answer immediately, Gaige gave a disgusted snort.

"It's because Claire is a woman."

"I'll deny that." Harry ran a hand through what little hair he had left. "But that's it in a nutshell. Gerald Preston hates that female reporters are allowed in the locker room. He refuses to have one in there that works for him."

"Egged on by Wally Compton."

Harry shrugged. It was no secret that the Knights owner and head trainer were old drinking buddies. What one wanted was usually reflected by the other.

"You didn't put up an argument?"

"I'm sorry, Logan." Harry's eyes were sad but resigned. "I have to pick my battles."

"That's it?" Logan asked after Harry was gone.

"I'll go to bat for her, Logan. Coleman's quarterback is not happy and I'm going to make sure he knows it."

"It won't do any good, will it?"

"No." Gaige put himself between Logan and the house. "Smashing your hand against the wall will only make things worse. Claire will still be without a job. So will you."

"Gaige is right."

Logan whipped his head around.

"Claire."

Logan didn't have to ask how much she heard. She looked... devastated. He moved to take her in his arms, his only thought to comfort her. Claire stepped back, shaking her head.

"I don't want to cry, Logan. If you touch me, I'm afraid I'll break into a million pieces."

"Break." Logan managed to keep his hands from reaching out. Barely. "I'll help you put the pieces back together."

"You can't. Not right now."

"I'm going to give you some time alone." Heeding Claire's wishes, Logan kept his distance. Like Logan, Gaige wanted to comfort her. However, a few hugs and some pat phrases were all he had to offer. It wasn't nearly enough.

"You know I'm here if you need anything."

"Thanks for not telling me you're sorry."

Gaige gave her a half-hearted smile.

"I let you down."

"Don't be an idiot." Claire felt a brief, welcome wave of heat. It wasn't enough to seep into the cold around her heart, but the burst of anger felt good. "You've been my champion. If you try to say different, I'll kick your ass."

"And you're just the woman to do it."

"What can I do?"

Claire shrugged. "Be the best damn running back in the game. Play your ass off. Win the Super Bowl."

"Okay."

It was such a simple response. Claire almost laughed.

"If I'd known you would be so agreeable, I would have asked you to top that off with the moon and the stars."

"There's nothing I wouldn't do for you." Logan took a deep breath. "I love you, Claire."

"Logan…"

"Lousy timing."

"No." Claire walked to the edge of the deck, her hands gripping the rail. "I love you, too."

Logan stood next to her. His hand was close to hers, not quite touching. "I pictured this moment differently. Flowers. Champagne. Me down on one knee."

"I pictured myself saying yes."

"That part doesn't have to change." Taking a chance, Logan brushed the side of her finger with his. When she didn't pull back, he curled his little finger around hers. "There are no guarantees, Claire."

"You got that right," Claire said under her breath. She hated that she couldn't control the tinge of bitterness.

"I was going to wait until I played that first game. My big, triumphant return." Logan had pictured in his mind a thousand times. This time, he saw a different ending. "I could get injured again."

"Yes."

Logan loved that Claire didn't sugarcoat it. Every time an athlete stepped onto a field, they were one hit away from the end of their career. Logan wasn't being handed immunity. He was lucky to be back in the game. That luck could turn in a heartbeat.

"I thought my life was over because I couldn't play football. It was everything. There was nothing I cared about after I was injured." Throwing caution to the wind, Logan pulled her into his arms. He tipped her chin so he could look into the deep blue eyes he loved.

They were sad, but he could see the love shining back.

"You showed me that there is more to life than football, Claire. I want to play. It's in my blood. But if something happens this time? I won't slink back to Denville. I won't hide behind a beard and long hair, and a bar."

"You're strong." Claire cupped his face with her hands. She kissed him with love – and regret. "Stronger than I am."

"Then, this time, let me be strong for both of us."

"You need to call your dad." Claire slipped from Logan's arm, backing toward the door. "Tell him your good news."

Logan felt a surge of panic as Claire slowly got farther and farther away. A few feet felt like miles. "Where are you going?"

"I need to be alone. To think about what I'm going to do." She paused, one hand on the doorframe. "I'm not leaving you."

"Promise?"

"What did I say the last time we had this conversation?"

"That I was stuck with you."

"Remember that."

"Claire." Logan called out. He thought she was gone. Then, just before he heard the front door close, she called out.

"Call your dad."

CLAIRE PUT THE key in the ignition of her beat-up Ford Focus. It was a hand-me-down of a hand-me-down. The best thing that could be said about the dull brown vehicle was that it had been dirt-cheap and it got her where she needed to go.

Now, she had no idea where that was.

Pinning all her dreams on one job hadn't been practical. It had always been a longshot. That didn't stop Claire from believing with all her heart that she would buck the odds. She had done it before. What was the chance a young woman from nowhere, with a few hundred dollars and one change of clothing, could come as far as she had?

Where was she now?

Then she heard the tiny voice. The same one that had guided her from Iowa to Seattle. The one that told her to believe in herself. It said, trust Gaige. Open your heart to Logan.

The message this time?

Stop feeling sorry for yourself. You have an education. Experience. Friends. And Logan. Never forget Logan.

Claire felt the weight lift from her shoulders. The ice around her heart cracked and then fell away. What was wrong with her? So she hadn't gotten the job with the Knights. There were other teams. Other opportunities. There wasn't another man like Logan Price.

She reached to turn off the ignition when the passenger door opened and the man himself slid in next to her.

"Hey."

"Hey." If there were any cold left in her body, the heat from Logan's smile would have melted it in an instant.

Claire grinned back.

"I love you." What else could she say? What else was there?

Logan wrapped her in his strong arms, his mouth covering hers. The kiss was classic. Long. Sexy. Oh, so satisfying.

"Where are we going?" Logan gave her one quick kiss on the end of her nose before buckling his seatbelt.

It seemed Claire had been asking herself that question all her life. *Where am I going?* Now, with Logan, it wasn't *I*, it was *we*. And she finally knew the answer.

"I don't care." Claire turned off the car. "As long as we go together."

EPILOGUE

L OGAN. LOGAN. LOGAN.

Logan closed his eyes, remembering every moment.

The chant from the crowd hadn't come at the beginning of the game, but at the end. Seconds left. On the two-yard line. The Knights down by four. Gaige handed him the ball. This time, he took it all the way for the score and the win.

"Still thinking about it?"

Claire snuggled closer. It was Thursday afternoon. Four days after the Knights season-opening home victory. The hoopla had faded. The team had Dallas to get ready for on Sunday. Logan was all business on the practice field and in the locker room. It was only game one. With fifteen more, they couldn't afford to look back – only forward.

"I think about it, too," she told him.

"Do you?"

"Only ten or twelve times a day. Aren't I allowed? The man I'm going to marry scored the winning touchdown. Don't I have the right to crow a little?"

"Damn straight." Logan tucked a long strand of her blond hair behind her ear, giving him access to his favorite spot. His teeth nipped at her neck. He was rewarded with Claire's moan of pleasure.

"Don't you want to know who I've been singing your praises to?" Claire arched her neck. She loved the feel of his lips. And his teeth. And his tongue.

"My father?"

"Mmm." Claire sighed. "Plus Rhonda and Pug. Between emails and texts, I think we've heard from half of Denville."

They were seated on the balcony of the newly rented downtown apartment. The plan was to find a house, but that could wait. They had all the time in the world.

"Tell me how many job offers you received today."

"Only five."

Logan chuckled. By his count, that made almost thirty. It was only right. The Knights had screwed Claire out of her dream job. Logan and Gaige decided they would do everything in their power to make the team sorry they let her slip away.

During the post-game press conference, questions flew at Logan. How did it feel to be back? Did he like the team's chances to take the division? How about the Super Bowl?

Logan gave the expected stock answers. He thanked the Knights for bringing him back. He gave all the credit to the coaching staff – his teammates. However, when he was asked what the secret was to his comeback, Logan didn't hold back. He made it clear he was there because of one person. Claire Thornton. By the time he left the podium, the entire country knew her name.

After Gaige spent a huge chunk of time extolling to the press the miraculous rehabilitation program Claire put Logan through, her phone started ringing off the hook.

Teams from every sport. Athletes. Hospitals. They all wanted to hire Claire.

Recognizing publicity gold, even Gerald Preston, the owner of Knights, had the nerve to offer Claire a job. Not as an assistant trainer. He wanted her *pretty face* in front of the camera extolling the virtues of her balms and creams. Products that Preston Enterprises would sell under the banner of the Knights.

Logan was so incensed he wanted to do the man physical harm after Claire showed him the text. She let him rant and threaten for several minutes. Then she reasoned that her best revenge was to ignore the man altogether. She planned to market her products, but Gerald Preston wouldn't see a dime from her years of hard work.

"You know I'll support whatever you choose to do. If you want to work for another team, I say go for it."

"It would mean me living in a different city for most of the year."

"We're strong enough to survive the separation. As long as you're happy, so am I."

"I love you." Claire kissed his cheek. "What I wouldn't love is waking up every morning without you next to me. A few days while the team is out of town, I can take. I'm not going to take a job in another city, Logan. But thank you for being so supportive."

"I won't lie," Logan said. "I'm glad you're staying in Seattle."

"I won't lie, either. I'm glad you're glad."

Claire knew what she wanted to do. She planned to do freelance work with individuals. Mostly athletes, since sports was her first love. However, if the right offer came along, she would be open to helping anyone who would benefit from her services.

"Some of those offers are pretty impressive. My contract with the Knights is basic. Will you mind making more money than your husband?"

"No." Most importantly, she knew Logan didn't mind. They were a team. That was all that mattered.

"Give it time. Next year, the Knights will have to pay through the nose to re-sign you."

Logan wasn't looking that far ahead. This was his time. Right now. Right here. Next year would take care of itself. The only thing on his mind was next week's game.

And Claire. Always, Claire.

COMING SOON

APRIL

AFTER ALL THESE YEARS (ONE PASS AWAY-BOOK TWO)

JUNE

AFTER THE FIRE (ONE PASS AWAY BOOK THREE)

HOW TO GET IN TOUCH

Please visit me at these sites, sign up for my newsletter, or leave a message.

http://www.maryjwilliams.net/home.html

https://www.facebook.com/pages/Mary-J-Williams/1561851657385417

https://twitter.com/maryjwilliams05

https://www.pinterest.com/maryj0675/

https://www.goodreads.com/author/show/5648619.Mary_J_Williams

www.ingramcontent.com/pod-product-compliance
Lightning Source LLC
Chambersburg PA
CBHW051245170626
46809CB00004B/1494